THE BLAST

*

A NOVEL BY

DAVID OHLE

The Blast

© David Ohle, 2014

ISBN: 978-1-940853-05-5

Small sections of *The Blast* appeared or will appear in different form in GIGANTIC.

designed by Cal Mari

published by Calamari Press
NY, NY

www.calamaripress.com

For Curly the black poodle.

Building the pedway so that everyone had access was a marvel of engineering. Yet no one knew who the engineers or builders were. They were lost to history. Though it was assumed that somewhere there must have been a central power source, perhaps in an underground facility with dynamos and belts and enormous gears, it had never been located.

It was near the end of the winter term at St. Cuthbert's Boys Academy, the only school still open in the township of Outerditch. Wencel, an honor student there, was known among the boys as Wencel the Pencil for his tall, bony frame, long neck and sharp, dark wit. He was out of bed early that morning. The great comet Velikovsky, brilliant in the heavens, shone through his bedroom window and woke him. Elsewhere in Outerditch, students anxiously slid Pop History and Emoticonics books into book bags while mothers darned socks and washed white uniforms.

Wencel went to his mother who was boiling grits and making johnny cakes on the brazier that morning and said, "Look at me. There is no hair on my face yet. They'll fuck me up at school for not having any. That's what they're doing now, the new administration. If you don't have hair on your face by the time you're a senior, you're fucked."

"Why would there be hair on your face at sixteen?"

"I'm at least eighteen, Mother. You forget everything."

"The hair will come in soon enough."

She served him a johnny cake on a saucer and a small bowl of grits. "If your father was here he would sort this out."

"He may never be here, Mother. You know how it is when you get sent to Altobello. You stay there ages."

Wencel ate the cake in an odd way by rolling it in his palms until it was a tight ball of oily dough then pushed it down his throat with a long thumb. The grits he spooned into his mouth, spilling some down his chin and dripping it onto his clean white school uniform.

"Close your mouth when you chew, Wencel."

"All right, Mother."

"And have faith. Your father will be back sooner or later. I don't remember much about him except he was mean. Heads will roll in the hallways at St. Cuth's. I promise."

"Mother, I've been up all night with the comet shining in the window and wondering if I'll ever get hair on my face. My father was there when the Blast happened. What if he gave me one of his bad genes? They all got them from the Blast, didn't they? We learned that in Pop History."

"You'll get hair. I think your father had a beard. I have a few hairs on my chin." She pulled on one of them.

Wencel leaned in close. "All right, Mother, I see the hair. I'm getting on the ped. School starts in an hour."

With his book bag over his shoulder, he went out to catch the ped going north to St. Cuthbert's. To do so he had to jump over a drainage ditch running south between his house and the pedway. It was a long leap for Wencel, even with a good start. There had been a wooden bridge there once, long ago rotted and fallen away. In early spring there would be a strong flow of snow melt in the ditch and the jump across would be that much more difficult. In early summer, after the rains and sometimes floods, the flow slowed and the leap was easier. Missing the bank, however, at any time of year and slipping down into the muddy bottom would lead to trouble at school. Showing up with muddy shoes or a wet uniform could get you a fucking up.

And there were a number of metal objects in the ditch along its length whose purpose or function was unknown. Some were wheels half as tall as Wencel, too heavy to lift. Others were misshapen globes, hollow, lighter, often fished from the ditch and used to kill sand rats, or as doorstops. It was commonly believed that they were the remains of a very old dismantled pedway dating back to the Age of Nerds.

When Wencel got onto the ped, he had to make his way past a little pack of white poodles and a pair of black ones. Poodles, sand rats and the occasional raccoon had learned to use the ped to get from one place to another. Why they wanted to go wherever they wanted to go was a mystery to Wencel. He recalled reading in one of his texts that in some far back era, animals like poodles and rats lived in well-defined habitats. They didn't move around from place to place by public conveyance or mix and mingle as they did now.

As the ped rolled through Bunkerville and Pisstown, the outlying townships, Wencel rehearsed his response to the fucking up he was sure to get. How would he explain himself to the power group at St. Cuthbert's, the senior "gate guards" with their full, black beards and muscled arms? Three of them stood at the arched entrance when he got off the ped in front of the academy along with several bearded young men. All but Wencel were waved on. Wencel lowered his face, hoping they wouldn't notice his very noticeably hairless cheeks and chin.

"Good morning Wencel the Pencil." It was Butch, the head guard. "Where's the hair? Half the year's over and you have nothing."

Wencel raised his head and closed his eyes. "It's coming in late. That's all I can say."

The three guards huddled a few feet away. Wencel cupped his ears but still couldn't hear them. He knew there would be trouble no matter what they were talking about. There was no hair on his face and that was that. The rules at St. Cuthbert's Boys Academy were rigid and unreasonable. If you didn't adhere to them, the guards would fuck you up.

Butch said, "Get on your knees and bend over so your ass is in the air and your head is touching the ground."

When Wencel did this, the crepe-soled bottoms of his school shoes were exposed. The guards could see that he had stepped in poodle shit on the ped, which enraged Butch, who shouted, "Somebody fuck him up right now!" The third guard stepped forward. "I'll do it." He kicked Wencel as hard as he could in the rear, pitching him forward, his head striking the brickwork.

Wencel stood up, pressing his hand against the rising welt on his head. "My father will be back and heads will roll."

"Fuck your father!" Butch barked. The guards chorused in their laughing. Butch raised a fist. "You see this? I could punch a hole through that bony chest and take your heart out." He called over the rest of the guards. "This boy needs some hair on his face." He pointed to a chair and a table set near the fountain. On it were a bowl of suds, scissors, a straight razor and a pot of glue. "Sit in the chair, Wencel."

A guard stood on tiptoe and cut Wencel's curly hair with dull, rusty scissors and collected it in a bucket. He then lathered and shaved Wencel's head, flinging the short hairs and soap from the razor to the ground. Butch used a brush to spread glue over Wencel's cheeks and chin then pressed clumps of hair from the bucket into it. The intentional result was a very poor approximation of a beard, clownish in aspect.

Butch slapped him to the ground. Other guards kicked him. "You've got a beard now, Pencil, so go to class."

With his rib cage throbbing from the blows, Wencel sat quietly in his introductory Emoticonics class, the front of his uniform shirt caked with glue.

The teacher, Father Bundt, neatly bearded, said, "Close all those dictionaries. We're having a quick quiz on the early use of Emo as a form of communication." He drew a single emoticon on the blackboard. "It's a bit primitive but there you are, one of the first ones ever recorded":

‹ 3

"Someone tell me what that means." There were no hands raised. "It means 'heart.' Come on, boys, Emo was the language of our ancestors. You must learn it to preserve it for future generations. Now, what about this one?" He drew another emoticon:

</3

"Boys, what does that signify?"

No hands were raised. Wencel knew the answer but couldn't speak. The drying glue had effectively sealed his lips.

Father Bundt went on. "It should be perfectly apparent. It means a broken heart. Now look, if ancient cultures were able to communicate with emoticons, so can we... What about this?"

(` } { `)

Finally a hand was raised: "Father, it means two people kissing."

"Excellent! And this?"

:$

Again, Wencel knew that it meant to blush or to be embarrassed but could say nothing comprehensible. No hands were raised.

"Good grief, boys, this is indeed an embarrassment." He looked around the room at all the hairy faces and noticed Wencel's false beard. "Oh, dear, look at Wencel. Isn't he a sight? The guards fucked him up pretty good. Well ... one more. It should be easy. Tell me what this one signifies."

:-x

Several hands went up. One boy answered, "My lips are sealed!"

"Correct," Father Bundt said.

*

On the ped ride home that evening, Wencel pulled some of the beard tufts free from his face and threw them over the side rail. Others remained stubbornly glued no matter how hard he tugged at them.

His mother gasped when she saw him.

"Look what they did, Mother. They'll do worse if I don't get hair soon."

"All right, Wence. Tomorrow we'll take the ped to Bunkerville and see Doctor Zanzetti. People at the souk rave about him. He's a first class folliculist."

"Does it hurt?"

"A little prick for every hair. Don't worry. We'll keep you dosed on metamine."

That night at bedtime Wencel's mother gave him a double dose, which quickly left him disembodied and cold. Shivering with anxiety, he got into his pajamas and settled into bed. She mopped his face with a cloth and warm water in an effort to dissolve the glue, and repeated the process every two hours all night until Wencel's face, red and raw, was free of glue and hair. She knew she would never get all the glue out of his uniform. Luckily there was a spare in the closet.

★

Bunkerville was a long ride by ped, but it was the only way other than taking a shortcut and walking all day along the icy ditch bank, ever careful not to slip and fall. Wencel felt like a sleepwalker that morning, his head still full of metamine, the comet flaring at him when he opened his eyes even just a slit. He sat down on the moving floor of the ped. His mother held his hand. "You'll get hair, Wence. This Doctor Zanzetti works miracles."

There were other St. Cuthbert's boys on the ped. Two or three of them were the very guards who had treated Wencel so viciously. As they passed him in a hurry, outpacing the speed of the ped, one of them spat at his feet. "Long neck. Pin head. You look like a mushroom."

"What's a mushroom?" One of the boys asked.

"I don't know. I saw pictures. They had stems and a head."

Wencel paid them very little mind.

Smooth-cheeked young men like Wencel sat in Doctor Zanzetti's waiting room showing wounds: black eyes, notched ears, missing teeth, broken noses, little pinpoint scars around their lips, bleeding scalps where clumps of hair had been ripped out like weeds.

After a half-day's wait, Wencel was called into the examining room. Against one wall was a display case housing examples of the doctor's work.

Most fascinating of all, Wencel thought, aside from the wispy-haired golf balls, was a human skull with a stringy black beard hanging from the jawbone.

"See," Wencel's mother said, pointing at the case, "If he can grow hair on those things..."

Zanzetti entered the examining room walking backward. "Excuse me, I always take as many steps back as I do forward. I'm not sure why. It happened after one of the forgettings."

As expected, there was a rich pile of dark hair on his head and a full grizzled beard. He turned and scooted over on a rolling stool and examined Wencel's face closely.

"How old is this boy?"

"Sixteen," Wencel's mother said, "Maybe seventeen or eighteen, even fifteen. It's hard to remember. He should be getting hair by now."

The doctor said, "It looks like the guards are giving him the business. I've seen this beard gluing before. Other insults and injuries, lip sewings. It's quite common at St. Cuthbert's. Not here in Bunkerville. Anyone here who needs a real beard can get one."

"They will torture him every day," Wencel's mother said, "until he has hair on his face. For now, that's their policy. I'm just a mother. What can I do? His father's been sent to Altobello."

Zanzetti cleared his throat. "Well, then, let's look over our chances here. The follicles are healthy enough. If we can get aggressive about stimulating them with the gun we'll have some hair production fairly soon."

Wencel tried to smile at the positive news, but his still sore, burning face prevented it.

Zanzetti produced the stiff pigskin mask from a cabinet. "This is the gun mask, son. I've put it together myself. Essentially it delivers bioballistic elemental particles into your facial cells. These particles contain genetic information, a simple message—grow hair. You'll feel a lot of hot little stings, and it'll all be over." He turned to Wencel's mother. "Has he had some metamine?"

"Yes, doctor. Two last night."

"Here's another." Zanzetti slid one into Wencel's mouth and whistled a disorganized tune for a few minutes, waiting for Wencel to fade out. After finding that a bore, he said to Wencel's mother, "All of my patients are boys now. You hardly ever see a grown man on the streets anymore, in any of the townships."

Wencel's mother said, "A lot of them were lost in the Blast and the rest were sent to Altobello. Wencel's father went there ages ago for stealing a crank radio from the souk. I barely remember him."

Zanzetti fitted the mask over Wencel's smiling face and turned to his mother. "Here we go." He pressed a foot pedal wired to the mask and a hundred searing *pips* could be heard. "That's the bioballistic particles going into the flesh."

When the mask was removed, Wencel's face showed a welter of bleeding dots.

"He'll be hurting for a while. Keep him on metamine. Expect some hair when the punctures heal in about a week."

"Thank you, doctor."

"To help with the healing, start with this." Zanzetti held out a cotton drawstring sack and opened the top to show small bales of dark, pressed hair. "It's a compound of various elements I've put together, heavy in potassium, a variety of nitrates. To counter the unpleasant odor of burning hair, I've added a bit of bergamot and Hungary water. You'll place one of these treated bales on the brazier until it begins to smoke and glow red. Inhale deeply through your nostrils as long as the bale lasts. Do this once a day, preferably before bed, and those cheeks'll heal in a week. In the meantime, stay away from school." Zanzetti patted Wencel's fanny. "Study at home. Not to worry. I'll send a letter to the abbot at St. Cuthbert's. He and I are close friends. I'll tell you a secret ... the abbot can thank me and the gene gun for that fine beard he has."

Wencel sat on his futon that night trying to study emoticonics in his dimly lit bedroom. In the kitchenette, with a pair of tongs, his mother held one of the hair bales over the brazier until it smoked, set it on her best china saucer, and brought it to him with a dose of metamine and a glass of water. He put the book aside. She backed toward the door. "Do what the doctor said. Take that metamine. I'm going to bed." She closed the door softly behind her.

The bale burned on the saucer in the center of the futon. Wencel's stomach turned at the odor of the smoke, which the added fragrances had failed to curb, and before long the cramped room was filled with it. He made an effort to breathe normally and draw in the ugly smoke. Soon he was asleep in a metamine gloom, and in the morning about dawn when he awoke and threw off the sheet, a cloud of fine ash burst into the air, a residue of the hair smoke.

On the sixth day of Zanzetti's treatment, after five with no sign of hair, Wencel awoke with a prickled cheek. He felt it with the palm of his hand. There was stubble. He shuffled from his futon into the *banyo* to rinse the settled ash off his face. When he did, his image in the mirror confirmed what he had felt. On his cheeks, on his chin, above his lips was a carpet of small, black, curled hairs. None were longer than an eyelash, but the gene gun was beginning to show results. When he presented himself to his mother, she was elated. "My goodness, that Dr. Zanzetti really is a magician."

On the seventh day, with clear evidence of healthy beard growth, Wencel returned to St. Cuthbert's. The guards were at their posts as usual. Students filed past them for inspection. The one in line behind Wencel had no facial hair. His cheeks were rosy and clear. Wencel didn't recognize him. He must have been a new student, a transfer from Bunkerville or somewhere.

"Well now," Butch said, "Wencel's been to Dr. Zanzetti. He's got a beard in the works, very sporty. I like that. Go on through. You'll be late for emo class."

Wencel took a few steps toward the quad, but turned back when he heard Butch shouting at the beardless new student. "Get on your knees, we're going to fuck you up."

Wencel lingered to watch one of the guards push the student to the ground and kneel on his chest while another pulled needle and string from a pocket. The student squealed when the needle was pushed through his bottom lip and screamed when the string was jerked through. Wencel couldn't bear watching any further. The lip sewing was a new tactic, the harshest yet. Before turning toward the fountain and the quad, he placed a hand on his cheek and moved it over the rooted stubble. He would always give credit to his mother for taking him to Zanzetti in time to avoid a lip-stitching.

*

Knowing that Father Bundt's Emo class always began promptly on the hour, Wencel turned and ran to the Language Arts Building and was seated in his desk a minute or two early. It was a good day for attendance. Only a few chairs were empty. Some of the boys were new. At the same time, a few of the old class members were not there. It was a thing that happened often at St. Cuthbert's. Students stopped attending and were never seen again on campus. Shortly there would be new students sitting at their desks.

Father Bundt arrived a few minutes late. "Boys, this is going to be a short class. I've been up all night. I'm spent. The abbot called a convocation of the faculty ... what's left of us anyway ... at three a.m. ... and another one in thirty minutes. There's a takeover in the works. He doesn't know when, but he knows it's coming.... So, as you might expect, I'm feeling very ..." He chalked an emoticon on the board:

>:(

One of the new boys spoke up. "You're feeling *angry*, sir."

"Correct. And I almost feel like ..." He chalked another emoticon on the board:

:'(

Once again Wencel knew the answer. "Crying," he said.

"Excellent, Wencel." Another emoticon went up on the board:

<:-|

Freddy said, "Stupid?"

Father Bundt was pleased. "Why are you boys so sharp today? Let me guess. It's because the winter holidays start tomorrow and you are all ... what?" The last emoticon of the term went up:

:-))

"Very happy," Berd said.

"Very good, Berd. Well, boys, including Roreg, Abers and Chitty, our new transfers from Pisstown, if we don't have a takeover, I'll be seeing you next term."

*

Wencel's father returned from Altobello the next day. A light snow had fallen. It was late afternoon, almost dark, when he rapped on the front door. Wencel's mother was busy in the kitchenette blowing on the brazier coals and preparing to grill krab as Wencel set the table for two. Both turned toward the door at the unfamiliar sound. Ordinarily, the only thing to be heard in Outerditch at that time of day was the *clatter-clack* of the ped going past and the chatter of its passengers on their way home from the souk and sometimes the sound of white poodles fighting.

"Let me in, it's cold." The voice was weak, a croak.

Wencel bent over and looked out the little front window. "It's a sick old man."

His mother came to look. "It's probably your father. He's back."

Wencel tapped on the windowpane. "He hasn't got a beard. They must have shaved him."

The father knocked again. "It's me, I'm home."

Wencel's mother seemed quite worried. "Let him in, Wencel. He must be hungry."

Wencel unlocked and opened the door. His father entered, stopping to shake off snow before dragging himself into the dinette. Still in the khaki "freedom" uniform and snap-brim cap everyone at Altobello wore, he collapsed onto a chair at the table as gaunt and thin as death eating a cracker.

Wencel's mother wiped her hands on a tea towel. "We're glad you're home at last, it seemed like forever. Look at that hair on your son's face."

"I see that, dear wife. It makes me proud. I won't be getting mine back. The follicles are dead, the roots are dead. How long have I been gone?"

She shrugged. "I don't recall."

"What was my name when they sent me off? Was it Jimmy?"

"I don't know. I know your face."

Wencel said, "It's kind of foggy, but I do remember when you and Mother took me to the beach at Point Blast."

"Did we?" his mother said.

"I can't forget Point Blast," his father said. "I was there when it happened."

Wencel's mother pinched her nostrils closed. Wencel did the same. There *was* quite an odor about his father, Wencel thought, mostly of sour, poorly washed clothes and mildewed cellar walls. A thin white paste leaked from his mouth. Wencel moved to the far end of the dinette table.

His mother said, "Well, you're here with us again, finally."

"To tell you the truth, I've been staying down there in the cellar for weeks, afraid to come to the front door. I finally got up the courage."

Wencel's mother sauced the krab, moved it onto a glass platter and served it. "I heard noises down there."

"I thought it was a rat," Wencel said. He set a third place for his father. "How did you get in down there?"

"A window well. I was careful, I was quiet, I didn't want to wake anyone up in the middle of the night. I scraped myself on the sill, but don't worry, I don't bleed anymore."

Wencel's mother said. "What's that white stuff you're drooling? It looks like toothpaste."

"I don't know, maybe pus. I've got abscesses in my mouth."

"Why don't you have a cold shower? It's right down the hall. I'll give you some scrubbing powder. And gargle, too. There's a water glass by the sink."

"The least bit of soap and water on my skin is like acid."

Wencel's mother passed the plate of krab to his father.

"I don't eat. I like the smell of food but I can't digest it, except licorice drops. I can suck on them."

Wencel leaned to within inches of his father's face, seeing now how leathery the skin was, how ancient the face seemed, quite older than it could possibly be. "Tell me about it, Father, what it was like over there? Was it worse than over here?"

"Not now. I'm dead tired."

"Where will you sleep?" Wencel's mother asked, but didn't wait for answer. "Not with me."

"Me either," Wencel said.

"I don't sleep. I'll stay down in the cellar. I like it there. I'll tap on the floor if I ever need anything."

Wencel's mother shook her head. "The *banyo* is up here. You'd be going up and down all night."

"I'm dried up. Kidneys don't work. I get a lot of gas but I can't remember the last time I went near a toilet. I'm fine, despite all. Forget about me. I'll stay down there all the time. Just give me a blanket from the closet. I can lie on the floor and think about things."

Wencel fetched a blanket from the closet and walked his father to the cellar door. "Good night, Father."

"Good night, Son."

Wencel looked down into the dark stairwell. "Father, there's no light. It needs a new filament. Mother will get one at the souk."

"I'm fine. I can see in the dark pretty good. I like the dark. Don't worry."

Wencel closed the door behind his father, who was so slight that the stairs failed to creak as he descended.

His mother said, "He shouldn't have stolen that radio from the souk. It got him sent away. And look what's come back. I hate radios. I never want one." She lifted a platter. "Have another johnny cake, Wencel. Let's not waste."

Wencel enjoyed another cake. His mother sat down and had a cup of gadafi, but didn't eat. "Even if he's in the cellar I'll smell him all the way upstairs."

"What about vinegar?" Wencel asked. He'd heard that would take odors away.

*

The spring term at St. Cuthbert's would begin in a few days and Wencel wasn't sleeping well. Aside from reoccurring dreams of the guards fucking him up, he was awakened time after time by the odor of death rising from the cellar. He went around groggy all day.

His mother said, "You don't look well, son."

"No sleep."

"It's the stink, isn't it, and all that teeth grinding? I can't sleep either. Sometimes I think we should just get a pair of pliers at the souk and pull his teeth. He won't feel it. He doesn't eat. Why does he need them?"

"All right, Mother, I'll pull his teeth."

"And I'll get a jug of vinegar from the souk and you'll sponge him down with it. I've heard you can brush them with shellac, too, and seal in the stink."

"All right, Mother, whatever is best."

Wencel went into the cellar to spend some time with his father the night before St. Cuthbert's resumed classes.

His mother shouted down the stairway, "Stuff something in his mouth to stop that grinding and put his blanket over him. Check for slugs. I found two on him this morning." She poured salt into his hand. "Give them a dose of this if you see any on him."

"All right, Mother."

Wencel, who always carried a handkerchief, stuffed it into his father's mouth and pulled the stained blanket up to his chin. "Be quiet, Mother needs her sleep. I need mine. Good night. Any slugs on you?"

Wencel's father turned his head. "A couple here on my neck."

Wencel fisted his hand and let the salt sprinkle down on the two slugs, waited while they shriveled, picked them off and stepped on them.

*

Wencel's mother was up at dawn making johnny cakes in the kitchenette. Wencel sat down at the table, his eyes ringed in red. "Good morning, Mother. I'm a bundle of nerves. I stuffed a hankie in his mouth but he must have spat it out."

"I heard grinding all night.... When you come home from school today, I want you to pull those teeth. I'll get a pair of pliers at the souk. And you can paint him, too. I'll get some shellac and a brush."

"I haven't studied enough for my Emo class."

"Here's a johnny cake and some grits. You want a cup of gadafi?"

"I can't eat anything or drink anything."

"Please, don't be like your father. Put something in your stomach."

"All right."

Wencel ate a bite of the johnny cake and took a sip of gadafi. "I've got to get on the ped. I'll be late for Emo. They'll crucify me. At least I've got the beard all squared away."

"It's beautiful, Son." She ran her long fingernails through it like the teeth of comb. "It isn't brushed very well, though. It looks slept on."

"I didn't sleep."

"You probably rolled over on it."

"Probably."

"Take a johnny cake with you. I'll put some dried krab in there, too. How can you go all day with nothing to eat? I'll wrap it and you can put it in your shoulder bag."

"All right."

Just as Wencel stepped onto the ped, three scruffy white poodles, sniffing the air, got off and trotted toward his house. It occurred to him that he had left the front door open and that his father's scent could readily alert a poodle. He dismissed the thought for the moment in favor of worrying about taking up classes again at St. Cuthbert's. There was a note of confidence even so, in that his beard would get him past Butch and his guards without a fucking up of some kind.

When he stepped off the ped with a crowd of other students in front of St.

Cuthbert's, the guards waited for them to file through. Butch was not among them. None of the old guards were. These were new and beardless. Their uniforms were different. No longer khaki slacks, black ties, fleece watch caps and shiny shoes, it was a clinical look—white shoes, heavily starched white canvas pants and jackets with red tri-corner hats tilted rakishly on the head.

A student whispered into Wencel's ear. "There was some kind of takeover. Father Bundt is dead. I heard about it on my crank radio, the Pisstown signal. They said it's nothing to worry about yet. But Emo class is canceled. The only classes we have now are Pop History, General Dramatics and Teleology."

Wencel's head sank toward his chest. "We don't have a radio. My mother forbids them. I hadn't heard."

"That's why you didn't shave, then. You don't know what happened. The word went out we had to shave. They're setting beards on fire."

A student ran toward the fountain in the middle of the quad with his beard in full flame, slapping at it, beating it with a notebook, trying to put it out. By the time he got to the fountain and dunked his head into the icy water, the stubble that was left was a smoldering ruin.

Wencel looked around at all the students. Most were shaven. Only two or three had beards. He looked again at the new guards and saw that they were all carrying cans of a flammable spray.

When it was Wencel's turn to stand before a guard for inspection, his heart beat so furiously he thought he might suffer an attack. He saw another student with his beard on fire running toward the fountain, screaming. The guard yanked on Wencel's beard, "What the fuck is this, you asshole? Don't you have a radio?"

"The truth is I don't. Mother won't allow it. She likes her quiet."

"Your mother? Fuck your mother." The guard sprayed Wencel's beard while an assistant held his elbows behind his back. Another guard lit a match.

"Let me go home and shave. Give me permission. I'll be back before the lunch bell, so help me Saint Cuthbert."

One of the professors stepped into the fray. It was George Flattering, who taught General Dramatics. "Wait. We need a bearded guy to play Saint

Cuthbert in the pageant. I wrote the play. It's only a couple of weeks away. He looks right for the part. Let him keep the hair. He'll be perfect."

The head guard said, "I hear you, sir." He poked Wencel in the chest with his finger. "Go to class. You won't be fucked up today."

Wencel waved at Professor Flattering. "Thank you. I'll be happy to be Saint Cuthbert in your play. Right now I'm late for my class."

Wencel walked past the fountain toward the registrar's office. One of the students with burned beards sat on the rim of the fountain, moaning. When he saw Wencel's beard he was puzzled.

Wencel said, "They let me keep it. I'm going to play Saint Cuthbert at the pageant."

The student shook his head and wept.

*

Wencel's mother heard poodles snarling and growling and tearing something in the cellar. She went down with a broom and chased three of them up the stairs and out the front door. Going down again, she saw the bottom of her husband's blanket ripped open and the stub of his foot showing through, the toes chewed off.

He tried to sit up. "Those damned white poodles got the toes on that foot."

"Wencel left the doors open again, the cellar and the front. I don't know what to do with him."

"I didn't feel it. It isn't bleeding. It's not a big problem."

"Whatever you say." She held her nose closed with a thumb and forefinger. "I'm going to the souk to get something to cover that stink. What if I'm not here some time and Wencel leaves the doors open and not three but ten poodles come in and eat your legs off?"

"I'll be fine. Go to the souk. Get me some licorice drops."

"We'll see if they have them."

*

At the registrar's office, Wencel sat in a metal chair beside a small wooden desk. An advisor behind the desk asked him questions.

"Name?"

"Wencel."

"No last name?"

"We're a traditional family. We don't use one. We can't remember it anyway."

"Don't you have a radio? How did they let you through with all that hair hanging on your face?"

"I'm playing Saint Cuthbert in the pageant. I suppose he had a beard like this."

"Yours is black, his was grey."

"It must have been black at some time or another, before it was grey. I'll be the young Saint Cuthbert."

The advisor tapped the card on his desk. "Normally you'd be taking Teleology One, but that's been canceled. Professor Billy was killed in the takeover. So you'll be in Pop History instead. This term it's a deep study of the Age of Sinatra."

"I know that period. Those were the days when Sinatra was singing and President Kenny was still alive."

"Room 3126, Building G-7. The class is taught by Professor Jerry."

"I'll do well in that."

*

With a late-winter chill in the air, Wencel's mother stepped onto the ped pulling a shopping trolley. It was a long ride to the souk and the ped moved slowly that day. The gears and bearings and belts were not being greased as they had been when the inter-township lines first opened for pedestrians. Maintenance had fallen away in hard times.

She got off at the souk with an idea for dinner, whole baked krab with sauce in celebration of Wencel's first day back at school. She felt sure that his beard would get him past the guards with ease. He would be in good spirits when he got home.

The krab vendor had a good supply.

"Give me two," she said. "Can you ice them? I have a long ride back."

"Sorry, no ice today. But the air is cool. They'll be fine in your trolley." He wrapped the krabs in waxed paper, then newsprint, and tied the package with a string. "Here you are, lady."

She lowered the krabs into her cart. "I'll need some sauce base, too. Do you have that?"

"It comes with the krab." He gave her a packet of red powder. "It's a little old. Mix it with water and boil it till it thickens. We bleed the krabs once a week and dry the blood."

"That's exactly what I want. I'm making a nice dinner for my son. He started back at St. Cuthbert's today. You should see his beard. It's prodigious."

"Goodness, gracious, lady. Don't you have a radio?"

"No, I hate them. I like the quiet. It's bad enough with the ped clanking by all night long."

"They've been burning beards there, setting them on fire. There were warnings on the radio about the takeover and the killings and the new dress codes."

"I don't take that seriously," Wencel's mother said. "The radio spreads rumors and lies." She moved on with her trolley toward the hardware shop where she bought a pair of pliers, a jar of vinegar and a can of shellac.

"We don't carry brushes, ma'am. You can smear it on with a rag.... Looks like you're going to pull some teeth, too. I had to do that with my daddy. I know how it is."

"My son and I, we can't sleep with the stink."

"It's a burden. But we bear it for loved ones, don't we?"

"Yes, we do." She loaded her purchases into the trolley. There was only one more thing to look for. "Do you know where I might find some licorice drops?"

"Three stalls down, Annie's Sweet Shop."

Professor Jerry stood outside the Pop History classroom greeting his students. He was a dark-skinned man with white streaks in his hair. He stood tall and weighed 300 or 400 pounds by Wencel's estimate and had a wide, gray beard that appeared singed at the bottom. He wore a black surplice and a three cornered hat.

"Good morning, sir. I'm Wencel."

"They let you in with a beard like that? They didn't set it on fire? You must be playing the younger Cuthbert. I'm going to be the older one." He drew his finger across the burned frizz of his beard's bottom. "They were doing faculty too. I doused mine in the fountain. *Then* they decide I'd make a fine *old* Cuthbert at the pageant, a little too late. Anyway, come in and take your seat."

Wencel entered the small, drafty classroom and sat in the front row. Other students followed, about a dozen in all. There were just six or seven desks, so some students had to stand or squat at the back where a half-open casement window let in frigid blasts of damp air.

Professor Jerry took his place behind a desk and rostrum made of cheap splinter board and called the roll: "Alert, Berd, Ellio, Freddy, Gordit, Lenny, Manx, Rogger, Randy, Sammy, Tem, Wencel and William."

All were present.

"All right, boys, listen.... In this class we're going to cover all the ages of history. There was a time, remember, when an age went on for quite a long time. And then what happened to change that? Anyone?"

"The comet came," Wencel said, "and then the Blast and then the forgettings, so time got compressed. Since then Ages go by much faster."

"Precisely. So let's get to the age we're going to look at first ... the Age of Sinatra. Why do we call it that?"

Ellio spoke up, "Because Sinatra was still singing then and President Kenny hadn't got that lead ball in his head yet from those shooters."

"Correct!" Professor Jerry rapped the podium with his knuckles for emphasis, drawing them back and looking at them, thinking he may have picked up a splinter.

Wencel raised his hand. "Sir, is it true that the Age of Sinatra came to an end when Michael Ratt was elected president?"

"Good question. Does anyone know the answer?"

Lenny raised his hand. "I don't."

Then came Rogger. "That could be said of the age, but Sinatra sang well into the Ratt years, so it's a fuzzy border. I'd say it ended when the Blast happened, about the time they raised the Titan from the ocean and hung all those survivors."

"Listen, boys. There are those who say that because of all the forgettings, real history has been lost. They say all we do is reconstruct the past from poorly remembered oral tales, the ruins we find, and the few texts that remain. Where is the proof that all those survivors raised with the long submerged Titan were hanged? What do you think?"

"It's a difficult thing to imagine," Tem said. "Why would so many survivors of a ship sunk by a blue whale be condemned to death? It defies logic."

"Loads of things defy logic," Wencel said. "Back in the Age of Sinatra, when people were enjoying a life without want or need, the Blast happened and all those bad genes were expressed, genes that still run in certain families. My father has it. He's in the cellar right now, pretty shriveled up. We have to keep him down there. It's quite an experience."

Allert said, "I've got an uncle like that in the attic. He doesn't eat much, but he likes licorice drops. He tells me all these great stories about the past. I like him. My father wants to bury him, but he's not dead enough my mother says."

Wencel said, "I like my father too. He went to Altobello."

"If you ask me, sir," Gordit said, "People with the gene problem are more adapted, more comfortable with their lives than we are. No pain, no striving, no need for food or drink, no urges other than licorice drops and resting. That seems pretty cozy to me, sir."

As Wencel was about to make a further observation about his father, the classroom door burst open and Professor Flattering strode in. He held his hands high and said, "Class is over. Except for the professor and that kid with the beard, the rest of you get on the ped and go home. We're starting rehearsals for the pageant."

Wencel and Professor Jerry followed Flattering down the hallway to an auditorium. On both sides of the entry door stood life-size statues of Saint Cuthbert; one as a youth, one as an old man. Inside, the domed ceiling rose thirty feet or more. Every sound from a footstep to a cough was muffled, yet clear, as if under water. Windows the length of the room looked out on the nearly frozen fountain and the frosty redbud trees that surrounded it.

In addition to Wencel and Professor Jerry, there were six or seven other students who had been selected to be in the play. Wencel knew a few of them, but had no idea where the others had come from. He had never seen them before.

Flattering climbed a few steps up to a chintz-curtained stage. "Boys, I'm Professor Flattering, master of general dramatics and stagecraft. As you know, the pageant play will be held in this auditorium on March twentieth, the feast day of our beloved patron saint. That gives us only two weeks to prepare.... Let's start out by asking, 'What do we know about the life of Saint Cuthbert?'"

Gordit said, "He was good. He helped the poor."

William said, "He was a hermit and he had a large member."

Wencel raised his hand. "He was born in Altobello in 1635 and died in Wyoming around 1780."

Flattering said, "True, true and true. We're off to a good start. Now, boys, I want you to read the play I've written for the occasion. It's called *The Life of Saint Cuthbert*. You'll get copies on your way out. We'll start by going over some lines tomorrow and seeing who'll be playing whom in the minor roles."

As the boys filed out, Professor Flattering distributed copies of *The Life*.

*

Annie's Sweet Shop had just closed when Wencel's mother got there. She could see Annie inside and rapped on the window. "Annie! Let me in. I need some licorice drops."

Annie came to the window licking nougat crumbs from her fingers. "Sorry, I'm closed."

"Please. My husband went to Altobello and came back half dead. The drops are all he wants."

"All right." In a moment or two she opened the door a few inches and slid a small bag of drops through. "Here, it's what I have left. I'll be making a new batch on Tuesday. Take them. No charge."

"Thank you, Annie, that's sweet. I'm not surprised you own a sweet shop."

Wencel's mother then stopped at a metamine vendor and asked for a hundred.

"They come in thirty-packs nowadays, ma'am. And we call them maximines now. They're stronger. You're dead to the world when you take them."

"Give me three then."

"Yes ma'am. You want the red ones, the blue ones or the white ones? They come in colors now, too."

"All right. One pack of each."

She pulled her trolley onto the southbound ped as a light snow began to fall. A black poodle got on and sat near her. Quite a few students boarded at the St. Cuthbert's stop. One of them, clean-shaven, leaned over and petted the dog. "These black ones are nice," he said. "They don't bite. Not like the white ones."

Wencel's mother wondered why the boy was going to school without a beard. "Won't you get in trouble? My son has a beard now. Isn't that the new rule?"

"No, ma'am. Today they were burning beards at school. There was a takeover. No beards allowed. The new guards set them on fire. Most of us heard about it on the radio and we shaved."

Wencel's mother weakened at the knees and did a kind of genuflection.

She couldn't catch her breath and fell into a faint until one of the students slapped her lightly and the poodle licked her face. "My poor son," she said, sitting up. "I wouldn't allow a radio in the house."

"They did let one guy through. He looked like Saint Cuthbert or something." He called to another student, "Hey, what's that guy's name? Hancel?"

"No, Wencel. Wencel the Pencil."

"That's my son."

"He was lucky, lady. He's going to be in the pageant. They needed a kid with a beard. Look at that boy down there. His got burned."

The boy stepped closer to Wencel's mother. She could smell the burned hair. Only a stubble of curled, uneven beard was left. "We didn't have a radio either. Somebody stole it."

"I'm sorry, son."

When Wencel's mother got off the ped at her stop, the poodle followed stealthily behind her. The ditch was dry enough now, before the thaw, that she could walk across and drag her trolley over the ice behind her. When she opened the front door, the poodle entered and ran down the cellar stairs.

*

Wencel was not far behind her on the ped with a broad grin on his face, happy to be the young Cuthbert and to be fully bearded. As tall and thin as he was, his gait, especially through ankle-deep wet snow, arms extended, was like that of a walking scarecrow. His mother, looking out from the kitchen window, readied herself to welcome him with congratulations. The krab was on the brazier, the pliers were set next to Wencel's plate, the father had been given his precious licorice drops, the poodle had taken up a vigil beside him, there was plenty of maximine and all seemed well.

The poodle came to the top of the cellar stairs when Wencel entered, watched him brush snow from his uniform, then turned and went back down.

"Mother, there's a poodle in the cellar. Did you know?"

"Yes, but this is a good black one. It's watching over your father. It licks that dry skin of his. We should feed it something so it won't be tempted to gnaw any more on him."

"All right, Mother. It's a black poodle. Back in the Age of Sinatra they called them dogs. They didn't understand as we do now that they were really poodles, not dogs." Wencel wondered what the emoticon for dog, or poodle, would look like. He imagined it would be a colon, numeral O, close parenthesis:

:O)

"What will we feed it?" his mother asked.

"I don't know, Mother. Sand rats, I guess. Please, I'll have a busy day tomorrow, rehearsals for the pageant. I'm going to be the young Cuthbert."

"I know. A boy on the ped told me. Congratulations." She served Wencel his krab with a nicely salted red broth over it and some wilted bitter weed on the side. She served herself a small square of krab.

Wencel forked off a corner of the krab. "And I also hear they're bringing in two female survivors from St. Dymphna's. Something happened over there. The rest were killed or poisoned by gas in a takeover. That will cause a lot of stress among the boys. It will be a nervous day."

"All that aside, son, I want you to catch some sand rats."

"This krab is bad, Mother. Feed this to the poodle. Can't we get some trotters? I hate krab every day."

"The souk has been out of trotters lately. As soon as you finish eating I want you to pull his teeth. I can't stand another night of that grinding. There's a can of shellac and a rag down there, too, and a bottle of vinegar."

Wencel burped, drank a little gadafi and took up the pliers. "I'll go do it. We both need the sleep." His mother gave him a lit candle. "There's not much light down there. We need a brighter bulb but you can't get them anymore."

When Wencel reached the bottom of the cellar stairs the poodle approached him only to sniff his shoes and cuffs. Wencel's father lay there with houseflies moving over his face until the poodle returned and swept them away with its short, fluffy tail.

On a sagging wooden shelf Wencel spotted the rag, the vinegar and the shellac.

"Hello, Father."

Wencel's father turned his head to the side with great difficulty. "Hello Wendell."

"Wencel."

"Wencel? That doesn't sound like a proper name."

"I got it after the last forgetting. Mother gave it to me."

"What was my name before I left? Was it Jimmy?"

"I don't know. Ages have passed since you went to Altobello. Things changed after the forgettings, especially names. We had to make up new ones."

Wencel showed his father the pliers. "Mother says I have to pull your teeth. She can't stand the grinding. Then I'm going to give you a vinegar treatment and a shellacking. Is that all right?"

"Go ahead. I don't care. Use your fingers. You don't need those pliers."

The teeth were so loose in their sockets that Wencel went right along pulling them by hand, one tooth after the next, all thirteen, with very little bleeding. He put them in his pocket.

Wencel tore the rag in half. He soaked one part with vinegar and dabbed it onto his father's dry flesh, as much as he could cover, until all the vinegar in the bottle was gone.

"That doesn't even sting," his father said.

"As soon as it dries, I'll do the shellacking."

In the time it took the vinegar to soak in and allow for a dry, shellac-ready surface, Wencel said to his father, "Everyone calls it the Blast. Was it really a blast, an explosion, or what?"

Wencel's father said, "I don't remember. It's all a haze."

Wencel dabbed his father with shellac, accidentally getting some of it into his open eye.

"Sorry, Father."

"It's all right, I don't care."

"Good night, then. It's good to see you have a poodle staying with you."

The poodle yawned, lay next to the cot and curled up to sleep.

*

The next day at St. Cuthbert's, Professor Jerry announced that the first female students ever to attend St. Cuthbert's, survivors of the St. Dymphna's accident, would be attending whatever classes were available. The girls were a bit under the weather after the gassing and looked ghastly pale, bug-eyed, frightened.

"Welcome them, boys. These are the Doolittle sisters, Daisy and Rosy."

The boys gawked at the sisters, smiled awkwardly and waved. Young females in the townships were rarely seen outdoors. Those who had the gene were kept in darkened rooms or cellars. The rest, the healthy ones, were sent off to St. Dymphna's, a school with a sturdy rock wall around it. They were permitted to roam the school grounds and play golf, but could never pass through the well-guarded gate.

Professor Jerry told the students to sit down and open their Pop History books to the chapter on the former president, Raymond Gunn. "By the way, who preceded Gunn in office?"

"Michael Ratt," Wencel said.

"Under what circumstances did Ratt leave office?"

"He was assassinated," Manx said.

"And how did that happen?"

Manx didn't know.

Daisy Doolittle raised her hand. "He was at a parade. A big balloon exploded over him. It blew his head right off."

Rosy said, "They blamed it on a guy named Oswaldo Ruben."

"That's right, girls, very good."

"Wait a minute," Sammy said. "How do we know any of that is true? What about all the forgettings? Everybody forgot everything."

"That's another chapter, the Forgettings. Yes, people forgot and most of them had hazy recollections and were too lazy to read the real history of the past. They found it easier to start from scratch and make up a new one. That's what we're studying here, popular history. It makes no nod to truth, as if any history ever did, but it's all we have."

Wencel raised his hand. "Sir, I'm going to have to leave class early today. We have rehearsals for the pageant."

"Not today, Wencel. Professor Flattering called in sick this morning. They said he was nearly dead. We'll wait and see. Listen to the radio. We may have to shave if the pageant's called off."

Wencel felt his beard, twisted it a little. He hoped he wouldn't have to shave. If he was awakened in the night, perhaps by his father's smell or a frightening dream, the beard was a comfort, a nest, between his face and the pillow. Without a radio, though, how would he know if the pageant was canceled?

He rode the ped that afternoon, on the lookout for sand rats. He knew they were slender, with prickly grey fur and webbed feet, slow moving, aimless. He'd seen them in great hoardes when his mother and father took him to the beach at Point Blast. He was nine or ten the one and only time they'd gone there. The following year the beach closed, overrun with rats, the sand covered with their droppings and skeletons.

When he got home and went into the kitchen he said, "All right, Mother, I didn't see any rats on the way."

"That poodle down there needs food. He's a good poodle, but if he gets too hungry ..."

Wencel had a fleeting mental picture of the poodle chewing on his father. "What about krab, Mother? Give him some krab."

"He doesn't like it. He turns away and whines. He doesn't like johnny cakes or grits, not even licorice drops. He wants meat, with muscle, blood and bones. I'm depending on you to find some."

"All right, Mother. I'll try again tomorrow. Right now I'm hungry."

He remembered then that his father's teeth were still in his pocket. He took them out and put them on the table. "What should we do with these?"

"I don't know," his mother said. "Throw them away."

He put them back in his pocket. "I'll keep them." His stomach growled with hunger.

His mother poured him a mug of gadafi. "The krab'll be ready in a while. Why don't you drink your gadafi then go down and see your father? He was asking about you today."

"By the way, Mother, the pageant could be canceled. Professor Flattering is deathly ill or something. If he is and it's canceled, I'll have to shave. It's a shame we don't have a radio. If we did I could know."

"Your father tried to steal one and look what happened. We will *never* have a radio in this house."

The poodle growled at Wencel's approach; a low growl, not a threat. It sat next to his father's cot, its shining coat as black as night. The dark eyes showed white in their corners when they moved, first from Wencel's father, then to Wencel, who knelt and extended his hand to the poodle.

"It's all right. You're a good poodle."

The poodle sniffed his fingertips, snorted and drew its muzzle into what might pass for a smile. All was well between Wencel and the poodle.

"Hello Father, it's Wencel."

The poodle licked his father's open eyes. "Oh, that feels so good," he said. "They get dry and they burn."

"You love that poodle, don't you, Father?"

"I call him Fleadle. He's my angel and he needs food. Please, get some." He extended his frail arm and stroked the poodle's back. "I don't want him to eat any more of me. Pull the blanket down, you'll see." Wencel lifted the blanket slowly away from his father. There was a smear of tissue and a little pool of grainy, brown blood on the cot. "Look, he chewed off my scrotal bag, so he's fed for the night. He'll need something else tomorrow."

"All right, Father."

At the table upstairs, as he ate his krab, Wencel said, "Even that good poodle ate his scrotal bag. I'm going to stomp some sand rats. When the snow melts they'll be swarming. It'll be a steady supply of food for the poodle. Where are Father's old golf shoes?"

"You know where they are, in the closet."

★

Wencel was up early the next morning, thinking he'd try to stomp some sand rats before going to school. Not wanting to leave spike pits in his mother's floor, he went outside in his sock feet carrying the old golf shoes, sat on the edge of the stoop and put them on. They were a size too small and his toes were cramped, but he didn't intend to stomp very long. It was already six a.m. He had to be at St. Cuthbert's by eight.

He got on the ped, thinking he would look over the side rail for sand rats. He knew they were often most vulnerable at dawn. Being more or less cold-blooded they would be stiff and sleepy then, easy to stomp. He saw a cluster of them a few stops down the line and got off with his shoes, almost missing the stop because of them. They had briefly become jammed in the moving pedway belt.

Once off, and a few yards into a bitter weed patch, he saw rats sleeping in pairs, cooing, dozens of them. He stomped five couples right away and realized he hadn't brought a bag to put them in. *I'm fucked*, he thought, then remembered he had four pockets in his school jacket. He put two in each pocket and carried the others by the tail and got back on the southbound ped looking forward to a good breakfast before whatever the day at St. Cuthbert's would bring. Without a radio to hear the news, he could easily get fucked.

His mother was waiting for him in the kitchenette with warm grits. He took off the golf shoes. "I've got some sand rats for Fleadle."

"That's good, Wence, here's your grits." They were steaming, a glistening white mound of them.

"Mother, I know they played a game called golf in the Age of Nerds, even before and after that. Father must have played the game. Look at the shoes."

"He found them in a dump, Wence. He stomped rats with them, that's all."

"What about the golf clubs in the closet?"

"I don't remember. He probably stole them from the souk."

As Wencel ate the grits, his mother stood at the top of the cellar stairs throwing rats down one at a time. "There you go, Fleadle."

Wencel heard the bones cracking as the poodle ate them.

★

At eight sharp the next morning, Wencel got off the ped at St. Cuthbert's. An array of guards, blackjacks in their pockets, stood elbow to elbow at the campus entrance. A line of students had formed there, waiting to be individually inspected. Either they were passed through or pulled out of the line and hit in the back of the head with a blackjack. Wencel averted his glance when he saw one of the guards striking a boy again and again with a blackjack. When he turned away he saw the Doolittle sisters in line behind him.

"Don't you have a radio?" Daisy asked.

"No, my mother won't allow it."

Rosy said, "We don't even have a mother and we had a radio. I've still got it." She held up a crank radio. "We can crank it and get some news."

"They're going to fuck you up," Daisy said, shaking a finger at his beard. "The pageant's canceled. Professor Flattering's almost dead enough to bury."

Wencel considered doing an about-face, running, getting on the ped and going home. He said, "I don't know what to do." He wondered if the guards would actually chase after him. He was twenty or thirty meters from the pedway. With his long legs he could be there in ten or twenty strides. And the line of guards was more or less the same distance off, and all of them were busy inspecting students, crowning them with their blackjacks or dragging them off to be fucked up further. He decided there was the opportunity to get away unnoticed. He would go home, scissor off most of his beard and shave the rest. He would use his father's old razor, the one he'd left behind when they took him off to Altobello. He would make lather with the krab oil soap his mother got from the souk once a month. Being late and beardless he would pass through with a rap on the knuckles rather than one on the head with a blackjack. He could be back at school in an hour, in time for Pop History. "I'm going to back away and go home," he said.

"Be careful, we like you," Rosy said.

Daisy winked at him.

He backpedaled half way to the ped, pivoted and walked slowly the rest of the way. In a few seconds he was on the ped without being seen and headed home. He looked back. The Doolittle sisters were waving at him.

When the ped passed the souk stop, his mother went by on the other track. He saw her getting off with her empty trolley to shop. He called out, but she didn't hear him with all the clanking and grinding of the ped's belts and chains, the barking of white poodles and the idle chat of souk-bound ped riders.

When he got home, he could hear his father coughing and spitting up in the cellar. He went down to check before starting the scissoring and shaving process. The poodle lay at the foot of the cot with a rat tail hanging from its bared teeth. The father drew urgent breaths, coughed up cottony balls of dry mucus and spat them at the wall.

"I don't have much time, Father. I have to shave my beard and get back to school. Is there something I can do for you before I go?"

"I need another coat of shellac. I'm beginning to stink again. It's bothering the poodle. It's bothering your mother."

"I don't have time now. I'll do it after school today."

"Fleadle needs more rats. He's hungry."

"I'll get some. But what's the urgency? Look at his belly. He's full of them."

The poodle yawned, curled its tongue then rested its snout on crossed paws.

Wencel shook with fear that he wouldn't make it back to St. Cuthbert's in time to save himself from a conking.

"Son, I want to tell you what happened to me in Altobello, in the freedom camp. They gave us jobs, we worked at this and that. Everything was extremely cheap. I sold used cars one time. A decent used Ford would go for six dollars."

"Please, Father. I don't even know what a Ford is. I will find out another time. If I don't shave and get back to St. Cuthbert's very quickly I'll be fucked."

Wencel paused a moment then rushed up the stairs and into the *banyo*, where he expected to find a familiar pair of scissors with tortoise shell handles in a cabinet drawer. They were not there. It was a very small *banyo*, not many places to look. His mother could have used them in the kitchen. He couldn't find them there. He went to the front door to see if his mother might be getting off the ped. She wasn't. He went back, made a handful of lather with krab oil soap and water and shaved the untrimmed beard with the old rusting razor, nicking himself several times, cutting more deeply twice on the chin.

He ran back to the ped and got on the northbound for St. Cuthbert's, his face bleeding. A little before the souk stop he saw his mother on the southbound ped going the other way. Her shopping trolley was full of string-tied parcels, sacks of grits, jars of sauce. He waved. She didn't see him.

Even an hour later, the Doolittle sisters were still in line to be admitted to the campus. Daisy put her hand on Wencel's shoulder and slightly squeezed. "They're conking a lot of people. It's taking time."

Rosy said, "You have a lot of cuts on your face." She dabbed the bleedings with a white handkerchief.

"It was an old razor."

"Word's been going up the line that Professor Jerry cut his throat trying to shave in a hurry with a sharp knife. He's dead. Mrs. Pillow will be substituting."

The Doolittles were waved through the gate by the guards without inspection, delay or detainment. It was as if they were invisible. They stopped a few yards beyond the gate to see what would happen to Wencel.

He was being talked to by one of the guards. "What are all those cuts on your face?"

He made up a lie. "I caught a sand rat and it scratched me."

"Not true. I know you. Did you shave in a hurry? You're the guy from the pageant, the young Cuthbert, right?"

"Yes, but I don't see that as an excuse to beat my head in."

The guard hit Wencel on the top of his head with a blackjack, stunning him. He knelt on the ground and rolled onto his back, the comet spinning like fireworks in the overcast sky.

"OK," the guard said. "Get to class."

Wencel staggered through the gate. The Doolittles took him by his elbows and walked him to Pop History.

Mrs. Pillow tapped a wooden pointer on the rostrum that sat on her desk. "Many scholars think zombies, so popular in the film and literature of the twenties, were fanciful depictions of the first Blast victims. But, students, I would say these are distinctly different beasts. Our victims today do not hunger after human livers or brains like the zombies did. Ours are harmless, so harmless we have to take care of them. Not that it's a chore ... they rarely want anything. Still, it's a burden for many."

"My father likes licorice drops," Wencel said, still a bit dizzy from the conking. "Sometimes they're hard to get."

"My mother's a real burden," Tem said. "She came home from Altobello a couple of weeks ago. We can't stand the smell. We're thinking of putting her out in the yard under some blankets."

"I can't live with the teeth grinding," Sammy said.

"They're easy to pull," Wencel said. "There's no feeling. I've saved my father's teeth and I plan to code them with emoticons and invent a game that uses them as tokens. And, if you want to stop the stink, paint them with shellac."

Mrs. Pillow said, "Enough about that.... There was a time during the presidency of Michael Ratt, a time that opened the door to the first forgettings, the takeover, all of which gave rise to the Age of Nerds." The students sat forward in their seats. "Then came the Illumination, a hundred years to the day after the great forgettings of the sixties and decades after the Age of Sinatra. So let's turn to page seven hundred and fifty of your Pop History books, *The Illumination*. Can anyone tell us anything about the Illumination?"

It was more than an uncomfortable minute before a guess was offered. Rosy raised her hand. "Did it start in about twenty-twenty when they had that big brainy conference in Bunkerville? All the smart people, the Council of Six were there. Maybe it was the Council of Three. I don't remember."

Mrs. Pillow folded her arms and paced back and forth across the room. "That's absolutely correct, Rosy. There weren't many smart people around then. Almost all had been sent to Altobello. And of course a lot of smartness in the population had been lost in the forgettings. So these few smart people suggested a change of course, a change that brought us here today, with almost everything in perfect balance, a society that finally works."

Freddy raised his hand and said, "I can't even imagine anything better than what we've got right now. Most of the people are gone, we live in these nicely isolated townships, we get everything we need to survive."

Wencel wasn't paying attention. His Pop History book was open to The Illumination, but he was scribbling ideas for the game he was designing that would use his father's teeth as tokens. It had occurred to him that with so many bad-gene people returning from Altobello, and so many teeth being pulled, a game using the teeth could be sold at the souk.

Turning the page to the chapter heading *The Bunkerville Conference: First Light*, Wencel began to sketch emoticons that would be painted or inked onto his father's teeth in his game plan:

: { = Sad
>: (= Angry
:' (= Crying
:') = Tears of Happiness
D :< = Horror
: / = Skeptical
: | = Indecision
0: --) = Angel
>;) = Evil

Before Wencel had finished sketching them all, Mrs. Pillow ended the class with the night's assignment: "For tomorrow's class, be prepared for a quiz on the Age of Nerds. Read chapter seventeen carefully."

*

When Wencel got home that afternoon his mother was in the cellar feeding the last of the rats to the poodle. She would say again and again, "Here, Fleadle, eat your rats. Here, Fleadle, eat your rats...."

Wencel sat at the table in the kitchenette with a pen and inked the emoticons he'd selected onto the teeth, which he held steady on the tabletop with a pair of tweezers as he worked.

His mother came up the stairs with rat hair on her chemise. "Wencel, we need more rats. Tomorrow won't be soon enough."

"All right, Mother."

She removed her chemise, bundled it and stuffed it into the laundry chute. "Some of your father's ribs broke through the skin. The bone is exposed. I'm not sure what to do."

Equally unsure, Wencel held the teeth in his closed palm, shook them, and slid three of them out onto the table. "Let's see what the teeth say."

"Why not throw all of them?"

"No, I've thought about it. The best way is to throw three at a time. You get better answers that way, simple answers."

He aligned the teeth and read the results: "Sad, crying and horror."

His mother said, "Throw three more."

"No, the next round you only throw two." He threw two randomly selected teeth onto the table and read the results: "Tears of happiness and indecision."

"So true," she said. "I don't think it's time to bury him yet, or maybe it is. I'm unsure about that. And I'll surely cry tears of happiness when it's all over."

"Mother, we can sell this game down at the souk. We can stock little emoticon stickers and the rules of the game. They supply their own teeth."

"Interesting idea, Wence, for another time. For now we need some rats. Trap some after school tomorrow."

"All right, Mother." He put the teeth back in his pocket.

"Go study. I'll make some krab."

Wencel went to his room and opened his Pop History text to *The Age of Nerds*. Although he looked at the words, stared at them, he didn't see them. He saw mental images of teeth inked with emoticons rolling onto tabletops all over the township, then at all the townships. He saw himself behind a booth at the souk selling illustrated, hand-written pamphlets called *The Rules of the Tooth Game* with a glossary of emoticons at the back. He was not going to abandon the game, no matter what. The rules would be quite complex, he thought, every casting of the teeth a revelation event, not all that different from the reading of bones or tea leaves. He remembered learning about those practices from the chapter on President Raymond Gunn, who held office eighteen-sixty to nineteen-sixty. The forgettings began in the last decades of his term.

*

Wencel saw only a few shoppers on the ped the next morning headed for the souk. There was a family of raccoons and a poodle, but no students. Normally there would be at least a few. He got off at the St. Cuthbert's stop alone. There were no students in sight. Beyond the weedy stretch of ground between the pedway and the school gates, he saw metal barriers painted bright red and a round yellow sign saying SCHOOL CLOSED.

He walked closer to the barrier, hoping for further information, but saw nothing more. He held up his Pop History text to shade his eyes from a bright spring sun and looked toward the fountain, which had been turned off. He didn't know what to do other than to get back on the ped and go home. Once again, the news had probably been broadcast and he had missed it.

On his way back to the ped, he heard a small voice behind him. It was Daisy Doolittle. She was running toward him, Rosy following at a slower pace. "Wencel, wait!" They were in their nightgowns, but wearing sturdy oxfords with red rubber heels, kicking up dirt as they ran.

When they caught up to him Daisy was breathless. "We were staying in the dorm. They turned off the lights, they closed it. They told us to get out. We were on our own."

"There's no place to stay," Rosy said.

Daisy extended her arm and squeezed Wencel's shoulder. "Can you help us?"

"How do you want me to help you?"

Daisy said, "We don't have a home to go to."

"That's a sad thing. You must be worried."

Rosy said, "We have to have food and shelter. You want us to starve and die of exposure? It's freezing out here at night."

"You're saying that you should be allowed to stay in my house?"

"Yes, and eat," Daisy said. "We like krab. Everybody's got krab."

Wencel drew his finger over his chin stubble. "I'll have to ask Mother. We don't have much room, about four hundred square feet, but we qualified for a dry cellar, luckily, because my father is down there now with bad genes and he's got a poodle named Fleadle. If you stayed with us, where would you sleep?"

"Rosy said, "Down there with him. I like helping those poor people."

Daisy said, "Let's go have a talk with your mother."

"All right."

The Doolittles took Wencel by his elbows and walked him to the ped. It was a twenty minute ride to his stop. On the way the sisters reviewed for Wencel what they remembered about the disaster at St. Dymphna's and the transfer to St. Cuthbert's.

"At St. Dymphna's we were in a dorm with fifty females. We wake up breathing air that smells like something rotten. Rosy and I, we're the first to get to the door and get out of there."

Rosy bowed her head. "Forty-eight died."

Wencel said, "They told *us* it was a sewer gas accident."

"No, it was something else, some other gas. It was a takeover," Daisy said. "It's the gene people. We could see them cruising at night around the dorm. We could smell them."

"How could that be?" Wencel asked. "My father is so frail he could never cruise. He can't walk, he can't stand. His ribs are breaking through."

"Wencel, you don't have a radio. If you did you would know from the Voice of Pisstown report that younger ones are coming back from Altobello now with a lot more energy and they're up to no good. First they closed St. Dymphna's with bad gas then they closed St. Cuthbert's some way or other. They took it over. They're sleeping in the dorms."

As if to validate Daisy's claim, a young male victim got on the ped at the souk stop with a brand new crank radio in his leathery hands. His face was a mud-colored mask of wrinkled flesh without expression. He wore the snap-brim cap and khaki uniform of a returnee from Altobello.

"You see," Daisy said, "there's one there."

"They have radios," Rosy said.

Wencel lightly slapped his forehead. "All right, all right, thank you for letting me know about all that, but I just remembered I was supposed to trap some rats today for Father's poodle. Can you help me? We'll just get off at the next stop and stomp some. It's easy. They're slow moving this time of year."

The Doolittles were willing. Their rubber-sole oxfords and stout legs would be perfect for stomping rats. The next stop happened to be at an open field of about a square acre. A farm boy had a stand there offering spinach. "Early spring spinach here, get it now."

Daisy said, "Wencel, let's get some spinach and bring it to your mother. We can have it with the krab."

"All right." He asked the boy, "Are there rats around here? Can we stomp some?"

"Help yourself. They eat half our spinach every year."

Wencel walked off into some brush and stomped one lying half asleep in a nest of dead grass. He put that one in a pocket. He stomped another, and another in quick fashion. Rosy, meanwhile, had joined him in the stomping. In a half hour they had stomped and pocketed seven. Daisy, meanwhile, carried a book bag half-stuffed with spinach. They said goodbye to the farm boy and got back on the ped.

All that while, the young victim rode on and got off at Wencel's stop. He had trouble getting across the ditch. All the joints in his body were dry and movement was limited. When he walked they could be heard scraping in their sockets. Rather than try to jump over the ditch, he chose to walk in small steps through it. The water was not deep, and was moving slowly.

He knocked at the door with a stone he found in the little garden, likely fearing that in his condition he might break a brittle knuckle or two by knocking with them.

Wencel's mother appeared at the kitchen window. She opened it. "What do you want? Who are you?"

"Jimmy Junior. Your husband's like a father to me. We knew one another over in Altobello. May I come in?"

"Just a minute. What is that? Is that a radio?"

"Yes ma'am. I got it at the souk. He always said he wanted a crank radio."

Jimmy Junior heard the lock slide open. Through a door crack Wencel's mother said, "It isn't stolen, is it?"

"No, ma'am." He produced a small bag of licorice drops. "I have some drops for him."

"All right, come in. He's down in the cellar."

Wencel's mother offered to make a cup of gadafi for the paper-skinned, dried out young man. "No, thanks, I don't drink anything anymore."

"You seem young to be that way, so far gone."

"Yes ma'am. It came on me fast. I was born in Altobello, so I caught it early. My father has it, but my mother was normal."

"Go on down. His days are dull. He'll be glad to see you."

Moments after Jimmy Junior closed the cellar door behind him, Wencel entered the front door followed by the Doolittles. His mother was busy pumping water at the sink for boiling krab and didn't see them until Wencel said, "They closed the school, Mother. They turned off the fountain and locked up the dorms. These girls don't have a place to stay."

"Some gene people took over, some young ones," Daisy said. They climbed over the wall and they gassed us."

Wencel's mother glanced over her shoulder at the girls in their nightgowns and oxfords. "That's odd because there's a young one in the cellar right now. He's a friend of your father's, Wencel, from over in Altobello."

The Doolittles gasped.

"Don't worry, girls. This one is very nice. I'm sure he didn't take over any schools."

Wencel pulled the rats out of his pockets and placed them on the table.

Rosy said, "I'll take them down. I'd like to meet this *nice* young one."

She picked up the rats by their tails, three or four in each hand. Wencel led her to the door and opened it.

Daisy thrust a bunch of what she thought was spinach toward Wencel's mother. "Look, we brought you some spinach."

"That's not spinach. It's bitter weed. I've seen that boy handing it out, the little slug. He hasn't got a brain in his head."

"All right, Mother, can these girls stay here for one night at least?"

"We don't have room. We'll be sleeping on top of one another."

"That's what I told them."

Daisy began to weep. "It's too cold out there with just these nightgowns."

Wencel put his hand on his mother's shoulder. "We should let them stay one night."

"All right then, one night. Tomorrow they get on the ped and go to Bunkerville. They have a home there for the wayward and the displaced."

"Mother, you forget. That home closed ages ago."

"Thank you," Daisy said. "I knew Wencel's mother would be nice. Wencel's nice, too. We really like him, my sister and me."

The krab water had reached a boil. Wencel's mother added a pinch of salt then used wooden tongs to place the krab chunks into it. Most of them sank to the bottom of the pot. A few floated on the surface. Those she pushed down with the tongs until they were sodden enough to sink. She said, "Wencel, go on down and see your father. I'll call you when the krab is ready."

Daisy said, "I'll stay up here and help with dinner."

Wencel went down into the cellar. There was only a guttering candle giving off a scattered light in the room. The poodle was eating a rat. Rosy sat cross-legged next to Wencel's father's cot. She had cranked the radio and it played old pop tunes at low volume as Wencel's father enthralled her with the story of his time in Altobello.

Jimmy Junior extended his hand to Wencel for a shake. "I'm Jimmy Junior. You must be Wencel. Your father and I were very close in the freedom camp."

Wencel shook a hand that looked and felt like a muddy gardener's glove, "Pleased to meet you, Jimmy Junior." He took notice of Jimmy Junior's height and general build. They were much the same as his. And even though the face was withered and drawn, there was a resemblance there, too.

Jimmy Junior whispered, "Please Wencel, listen to your father. In a roundabout way he's telling us something we need to know."

"But Mother is fixing krab. It'll be ready in a few—"

Rosy placed a forefinger across her lips. "*Shhhh.*"

The poodle, with a rat in its mouth, growled.

"All right." Wencel leaned against the wall, folded his arms and listened.

Jimmy Junior pushed a licorice drop into Wencel's father's mouth. "Here, if you're going to be talking, you need some lubrication."

"Thank you, son.... Like I was telling Rosy here and Junior, summers in Altobello were hell. It never rained. Every day the sun got stuck up there and stayed for hours. It was so hot one Friday, the asphalt lot at Altobello Motor Sales had begun to bubble. That's where I was working at the time. Everybody over there had jobs. I was selling used cars, cheap cars. A fairly good one would go for two or three dollars. We didn't get paid much, but everything was dirt cheap.

"So there I am that Friday in my little air-conditioned sales hut and I lean back in my chair, thinking about taking a nap, and I hear voices in the lot, a different language. When I stand up and go to the window, I see pale, dark-haired men standing around a pricey, vintage '78 Cadillac. They look like new arrivals, possibly Russian, possibly Bosnian. Dressed old-fashioned, they surround the car, giving it a serious once-over. One of them wipes dust from a headlight with a handkerchief.

"I open the little window and yell, 'Quit ogling the fucking thing and give me ten bucks. You can drive it away right now.'

"'We just look,' one of them says, opening the door and getting into the driver's seat. He moves the steering wheel back and forth playfully.

"I decide I'm going to chase them away. By the time I open the door and step down onto the soft asphalt, blinded by windshield reflections, the men are gone, as if they'd been an apparition, as if they'd stepped into another dimension. I wondered if it had been a particularly realistic daydream. Or were they hiding somewhere among the cars? I look under them, I look behind them. All I see is a scrawny poodle chewing on a dead cat."

"I've never seen a cat," Rosy said. "Didn't they die out?"

"Here, maybe. Over there there's a lot of cats and no rats."

Wencel's mother tapped the floor with the bottom end of her broom handle. "The krab is ready! If you're hungry, come up and eat."

Wencel's stomach was empty and making noises. "I'm going up. Rosy, are you coming?"

She turned off the radio. "I haven't eaten since yesterday. I'm coming."

Jimmy Junior said, "I'll stay here with him. I don't need to eat."

Wencel said, "All right, Father, we'll come down and listen after supper."

Rosy said, "I think I'll sleep down here on the floor if I can get a blanket upstairs."

"I will, too," Jimmy Junior said. "I don't need a blanket."

Wencel's mother served bowls of krab in clear broth and had set out spoons for everyone at a small metal table that barely seated four. Those in the side seats, Daisy and Wencel, were close enough to tangle arms and elbows as they dipped krab broth. Rosy and Wencel's mother, at the ends, were freer in their movements.

Wencel's mother said, "Well, Wence, I've grown to like Daisy here quite a lot. She can sleep in my bed. It's wide enough."

Rosy said, "Is there a blanket I can have? I'll bed down in the cellar."

Wencel's mother said, "In the closet down the hall. It's a wool one from my husband's Army days. He was serving down at Point Blast. He was there when it happened."

"Oh, goodness," Rosy said, "That's very sad." She finished the last of her krab and asked to be excused. She padded along the hallway, feeling her way in the dim light for the closet door.

Wencel's mother called after her, "Be careful. There's an old golf bag in there, and clubs. Don't let them fall on you."

When Rosy's fingers curled around the closet knob, she opened the door, letting in a little of the hallway light, enough to see the golf bag on the top shelf, some of the clubs thrust halfway out. As she pulled the blanket out and into her arms she was careful not to touch or bump anything for fear the clubs would rain down on her head.

As she passed the kitchenette on her way to the cellar door, Wencel's mother said, "My husband was a golfer before the Blast. After the Blast, and the forgettings, he was too stupid to play."

When Rosy had gone down the stairs and Wencel had eaten his fill of krab, he said, "Mother, Father is telling a story about Altobello. Jimmy Junior says I should hear it. Would you like to come down with me and listen?"

"No, the kitchenette needs cleaning. You go and listen."

"Daisy?"

Daisy and Wencel's mother looked at one another for a moment.

Daisy said, "I'll stay up here and help your mother clean the kitchenette."

Wencel went down. Rosy and Jimmy Junior knelt beside Wencel's father's cot. A small portion of the comet's light coming through the cellar window and a small candle let Wencel see where he was going. He assumed his position, leaning against the damp wall.

His father's tongue protruded unnaturally and was utterly white. His eyes were closed. A throaty wheeze came from his throat.

Jimmy Junior said. "That's the rattle. The story is over. He's dead enough to bury now. It's time to make plans, brother. Go up and talk to your mother. I'll be right behind you."

"Talk to my mother about what?"

"The burial ... of *our* father."

"I don't understand what you mean. I do remember something from Pop History, though, about an old cult of Extians during Michael Ratt's time who had an incantation that went something like, 'Our Father whose art is heavy, we worship you' ... something like that?"

Rosy wept.

Jimmy Junior said, "Wencel, go up and tell your mother to make a pot of strong gadafi. We have things to talk about. We'll meet in the kitchenette."

Wencel turned around. "All right." He went up the stairs, ducking his head to keep it from hitting the low ceiling.

Jimmy Junior said, "I'm right behind you. Don't fall backward."

When Wencel got to the kitchenette Daisy was sitting at the table eating a johnny cake.

"Mother, Jimmy Junior here wants to have a meeting."

"A *family* meeting," Jimmy Junior said. "I suggest you make a pot of strong gadafi for the rest of you. I don't want any."

"All right." Wencel's mother felt Jimmy Junior's urgency. She spooned gadafi powder into a saucepan, filled it with pumped water and set it on the brazier to boil.

Wencel said, "We should tell you, Mother, Father is dead enough to bury now."

"It has to be done quickly," Jimmy Junior said.

"I *thought* I heard weeping down there," Daisy said.

Wencel's mother stirred the gadafi. "We'll make plans. We'll get him in the ground."

"The ground is half-frozen," Wencel said. "And we don't have a shovel anyway."

"Let's burn him," Daisy said.

Wencel said, "There's nothing to burn around here."

"Not even a stick," his mother said. She served bowls of krab to Wencel and Daisy.

"Let's eat and talk later," Wencel said.

"Yes, let's," Daisy said.

Wencel's mother said, "You girls can't go around in those nightgowns. I have some outfits in the closet you can wear."

When the krab was eaten and everyone had a cup of gadafi in front of them, Jimmy Junior said to Wencel's mother, "I'll be blunt. I'm Wencel's half-brother. Your husband, Jimmy, mated with my mother, fathered me and at the same time, passed on the gene. You could think of me as Wencel's dead brother."

Wencel's face brightened. "I think there was a singer back in the Age of Sinatra who had a dead brother. His name was Jesse Pelvis."

Wencel's mother sighed. "I think it's all very good that Wencel has a brother. I'm sorry you have the gene, Jimmy Junior."

"Tough luck," Wencel said. "I'm glad I don't have it."

At this moment, the meeting was interrupted by Rosy running up the stairs, bursting through the door, cranking the radio. "Wencel, Daisy! It's on the Voice of Pisstown Report. St. Cuthbert's is open again! Tomorrow!"

"Then we'll have to do something with Father tonight," Jimmy Junior said. "If we can't bury him and we can't burn him up, what can we do?"

Wencel said, "There's some water in the ditch. The snow is melting. Father's pretty dry, he'll float."

Wencel's mother said, "All right. Wencel, you go down and bring him up. He's not very heavy."

"Girls, go get some warmer clothes from the closet."

"What about the poodle?" Daisy asked.

"He's free to go," Wencel's mother said.

Rosy opened the cellar door and Wencel went down. His father was no heavier than a bundle of sticks. Lifting him was not a strain at all. The poodle yawned, pawed the floor then followed Wencel, who carried his father up the stairs. It sat near the kitchenette wagging its tongue, as if waiting for further action.

A procession soon made its way to the ditch: Wencel carrying his father, followed by his mother. Daisy and Rosy, both wearing Wencel's mother's old sweaters and jumpers, followed them. Jimmy Junior and the poodle were last. There was enough light falling from the comet to show the way. At the edge of the ditch, as Wencel held his father over the water, Jimmy Junior stepped forward. "Wencel, hold him, I have a few words to say."

"All right," Wencel said, getting a better footing on the bank. Slipping in would be a disaster.

Jimmy Junior raised his hand toward the sky. "The great comet will guide him to a place of rest. Gloria hoopla, Wencel, let him get on down the road. Drop him into the water."

Wencel lowered him without getting his feet wet and placed his father in the ditch water. The current took him rapidly for a short distance, where he snagged on a hunk of rusted metal and came to a stop. "He's stuck," Wencel's mother said. "Somebody get in the ditch and set him loose."

"Not me," Wencel said. "That water's cold."

"I'll do it," Rosy said. But before she could move a step, the poodle leapt into the water, up to its belly, and nudged the Father with its snout until he was free and on his way downstream. After looking up for a moment at the group on the bank, the poodle gave way to the current and let itself be swept away behind the Father.

As the group trudged back to the house, Rosy wept. Daisy and Wencel's mother walked hand in hand. Wencel tried to put his arm over Jimmy Junior's shoulders as a gesture of affection, but it was rejected. "No, brother, you might break some bones."

*

That night Daisy and Wencel's mother slept in Wencel's mother's bed. Wencel slept on his futon, Rosy on a blanket in the cellar beside Wencel's father's cot. Jimmy Junior lay beside her. "I don't really sleep anymore," he said, "but I do grind my teeth while I'm lying awake."

Rosy said, "I won't be bothered. My father did it every night. He had what you have."

"I'll be leaving tomorrow, Rosy, going to Point Blast. The warm sun down there and the sea air ... it's all good for me."

"I don't want you to go, Jimmy Junior. I like you."

"Come with me. They tell me you can just move into one of the empty cabins, the ones that survived the Blast. Nobody's lived in them forever."

"Will you let me take care of you? You're so dry. Aren't you afraid you'll be burned by the sun? We'll get some oil and I'll oil you down."

"The view of the comet from Point Blast is something to be seen before you die. It fills the sky at night much more than it does here."

The next morning, Daisy and Wencel's mother were up early, brewing gadafi and boiling grits. As they moved back and forth from sink to brazier, they sometimes stopped to embrace.

The comet's light through the oval window in Wencel's room awakened him. His first feeling was one of relief that his father was dead and gone and that the poodle had chosen to go with him. His going was more of a gain than a loss, to think about it rationally. There would be no need to stomp rats any longer, or shellac him or anything else.

The smell of gadafi and grits brought him off the futon and into the dinette.

"Good morning, Mother. Good morning, Daisy. The comet is very bright today, a good sign for going back to school."

Daisy served him a mug of gadafi and a bowl of grits. She said, "I'm not going back. Your mother and I are going to have a child. I'll be exempt from school when I'm pregnant."

Wencel's mother came to tears, "I want a grandchild, Wence. Daisy will be the mother."

Wencel sipped his gadafi and thought for a moment. "And the father?"

"You, Wencel," Daisy said. "That's what a grandchild is, isn't it?"

Before the conversation went any further, Rosy and Jimmy Junior came up from the cellar and sat at the dinette. Rosy lowered the crank radio to the floor.

Wencel's mother ladled grits into a bowl. "Grits, Rosy? Gadafi?"

"Please, yes, I'm starving and half asleep. I didn't get much last night."

"It was my grinding," Jimmy Junior said. He smiled at Rosy, cracking the corners of his lips in the process. "She said she didn't mind, but she was lying."

Rosy smiled back, gently passing two fingers over his cheek. "Jimmy Junior and I are going to Point Blast. I'll be taking care of him till the end."

"Not that I need care-taking. I don't *need* anything."

Rosy playfully shook a finger at him. "Other than licorice drops ... and don't forget shellacking. You'll need that before long, and those teeth will have to be pulled sooner or later." She turned to Wencel's mother and Daisy. "He really needs me."

Daisy hugged her sister. "I've got news, too. I'm going to have Wencel's child."

Wencel's mother sipped her gadafi. "My grandchild."

"All that is ducky," Jimmy Junior said, "but we've got to get an early start. It's a long ride to the Point."

Wencel raised his head. He had lowered it to give himself a chance to think over the things he was hearing. For one, he had only a foggy idea of how to mate with a female. There had been nighttime discharges from his member, a thick white gel with a light chemical odor, accompanied by a delightful sensation. He knew this was a key part of mating and producing offspring.

In only an hour he would have to be arriving at St. Cuthbert's. He had to put on his uniform, shave with his father's old razor, buff his shoes with a soft cloth, do his toileting and catch the ped.

Wencel said, "I'm sorry. I have to get ready for school." He finished his gadafi and grits and disappeared down the hall in his slippers and pajamas.

"I should tell him what I heard on the radio before he goes," Rosy said.

Wencel's mother said, "Not another takeover I hope. Wencel has been fucked up enough."

"Not a takeover," Rosy said. "It's more like a shakeup. Some heads rolled. No one knows what to expect."

Jimmy Junior was growing agitated, pulling small tufts of hair, grinding his teeth.

Rosy said, "We have to go. Look at him." She stood and helped him to his feet. "Should I leave the radio?"

Jimmy Junior said, "Yes, leave it here. It's rightly theirs."

"I like radios," Daisy said.

Wencel appeared in uniform with his book bag. "Mother, can we finally have a radio? Father's dead. Let's pardon him for stealing one once."

"All right," his mother said. "Leave it."

On her way to the front door, Rosy said, "Good luck at school, Wencel."

Wencel walked with them to the ped. Jimmy Junior couldn't jump the ditch and had to wade across with Rosy and Wencel on either bank holding his hands.

"Good bye, Jimmy Junior. Goodbye Rosy."

Standing on tiptoe, Rosy gave Wencel a little buss on his cheek. "Come visit sometime."

"I will."

"Bring the grandchild."

Rosy and Jimmy Junior stepped onto the southbound Point Blast ped and Wencel stepped onto the northbound St. Cuthbert's ped.

When he arrived at the stop he was surprised to see no guards on duty. The entrance gate was wide open. A few of the fountain's spigots spurted water, others remained frozen. About twenty students in uniform milled around it, talking, laughing, roughhousing. Some had beards of varying length. These were new students. Wencel had never seen them before.

"Where are you from?" he asked them.

"They brought us up from Point Blast. St. Gilbert's got blown up. So here we are. Didn't you hear about it on the radio?"

"No, I didn't. But I do have a radio now, at last. I was told the Pisstown report said to expect anything today."

"We don't know what to expect either." Three of the new Point Blast students introduced themselves as Bubba, Penta and Day.

"I'm Wencel."

Penta asked, "What're the best courses to take?"

"I like Pop History. General Dramatics is good too. But the teacher might be very sick."

Day asked, "Are there females here from St. Dymphna's? I don't see any around."

"No, not any more. There were only two. One went with my half-brother to Point Blast, the other one will be the mother of my mother's grandchild. They say I'll be the father. She's staying with us."

The new boys looked at one another. Bubba said, "You got a house, Wencel?"

"I do. It's my mother's house."

"Is it wooden?"

"The top is wooden, the cellar is stone. It's about an hour down the ped."

The boys huddled and chatted in low tones, away from Wencel. When the huddle broke, Penta said, "The three of us, we don't have a place to live. The school is open but the dormitories are closed for maintenance. What would you say to us coming out there and staying for a night or two?"

"Oh, no, we don't have room. I'm sorry."

The assembly bell rang and Wencel took off toward the Language Arts Building, hoping never to run into the three new boys again and to dodge the question of them staying in his mother's house, which would be unbearable under the circumstances.

In the foyer there were three available courses listed on a bulletin board: Pop History—Room 121 (8:00), General Dramatics—Auditorium (9:00), Teleology—Sub-Level 2 (10:15).

Wencel decided to take all three.

*

Daisy and Wencel's mother took the ped to the souk to get a few things.

"I'm hoping they have some trotters at least," Wencel's mother said. "We haven't had any meat for a while. I'm a little sick of krab."

"I have a sudden yen for licorice drops," Daisy said. "Let's get some at the candy shop."

"All right."

Wencel's mother hoped this was just a sweet tooth talking and not a sign that Daisy was expressing a problem with her genes. She didn't want a half-dead grandchild.

At this early hour there were not many people at the souk, the lines at all the booths short. Pinned to the canvas overhang of one of the booths was a sign that said: TROTTERS TODAY—OUT OF KRAB.

"Oh, look, Daisy, trotters today." Wencel's mother hurried to the booth, dragging her shopping trolley behind. There were only three or four shoppers in front of her. A big steaming pot of boiling trotters sat on the brazier. A vendor dipped them out three at a time and wrapped them in waxed paper. "Here you go, ladies." He gave a bundle to everyone in the line. Daisy and Wencel's mother were last and therefore got the two extra that were left in the pot. "Some lagniappe for you two. Enjoy these with red beans. They've got some over there." He pointed to a booth down the way with buckets of beans on display, white, brown, black and red. "Big harvest down around Bunkerville last summer."

Wencel's mother put the wrapped trotters into her shopping trolley and said to Daisy, almost tearfully, "I do hope Wencel isn't getting fucked up at school today."

Daisy clapped her hands. "We'll make him a nice dinner when he gets home. Trotters and beans, not grits, no krab."

On the way to the bean booth, they passed a vendor selling bitter weed wine. "Homemade, home bottled," the vendor said, "very strong."

"I haven't had wine in years," Wencel's mother said.

"Let's get a bottle," Daisy said, "to go with the trotters."

The bottles, sealed with paraffin, lay on a metal folding table. Had Wencel been there he would have been able to identify the table as an artifact from the Age of Sinatra, then called a card or game table.

Daisy lifted one and placed it in the shopping cart.

"Get another one," Wencel's mother said. "We need to relax Wencel if we expect to get him to mate with you. He doesn't know how."

"I think I do," Daisy said. "We read about it at St. Dymphna's. I'll show him."

There was another stop at a vendor offering hand-made jumpers in several colors and an assortment of twill blouses. "I'll get a blue jumper with a white blouse," Daisy said. "I'll look nice for the mating."

*

On the ped, approaching Bunkerville, a white poodle nipped off one of Jimmy Junior's fingers and ran away crunching bone. "They can smell me, Rosy. I'm going to need a shellacking."

Rosy sucked what little blood came from the stump.

"Jimmy Junior, you're exhausted. We should stop and rest."

His spindled legs had lost all sensation. He was about to crumble into a heap. Rosy leaned against his shoulder to keep him from falling sideways. If he pitched forward, she held him up by grasping the back of his canvas belt. "Let's get off and rest awhile in Bunkerville," she said.

The place to rest nearest the Bunkerville stop was a small café, the Squat 'n' Gobble. While Jimmy Junior stood outside, Rosy went in and asked the attendant if bad gene types were allowed in.

"Why should we, lady, when they don't eat or drink?"

"He only wants to rest. I'll have some gadafi and a johnny cake."

"Okay, let the poor bugger in."

Rosy opened the door, led Jimmy Junior to a table and sat him down. The café was a warm, comfortable place with the brazier going in the kitchen and the smell of gadafi brewing. It was an odd time between lunch and dinner, so there were few other diners. Two sat at another table and three or four squatted on low stools at the counter slurping trotter soup. Otherwise there were dozens of empty tables and booths.

Rosy sipped gadafi and ate a johnny cake.

Jimmy Junior stared at the diners at the counter for a moment. "I wonder what happens to the rest of the animal. The feet are eaten but what kind of animal is it, a pig? Have you ever seen a pig, a pig on the hoof?"

"No, but I've heard of them."

"Fat little meaty animals eaten back when. If they're raising them again, slaughtering, butchering and eating them, where is all the meat going? We see the feet, not the meat."

"You know a lot of history, Jimmy Junior, like Wencel does."

"Wencel went to school. There were no schools in Altobello. My father taught me to read and write. I read a few books, too, like *The Age of Sinatra*. I learned a lot of real history from that."

The waitress came to the table. "Anything else? Another gadafi?"

"No thank you," Rosy said.

The waitress placed a licorice drop in front of Jimmy Junior. "Here you go. The cook said to give you this."

The cook waved and smiled from the kitchen.

"Where you two headed?" the waitress asked.

"The Point," Rosy said. "We're going to live there. The salt air will do him good. He says he wants to live out his time listening to the roar of the water and breathing salty air."

Jimmy Junior said, "I feel good in spirit, you know, but my body's bad. So, we're going there no matter what for however long."

About dusk, Rosy and Jimmy Junior left the café. Among Jimmy Junior's many afflictions was night blindness. "I can't see," he said.

Rosy held his hand. "Follow me."

★

Wencel took a seat in Room 121. He was a few minutes early and for a while was the only one there. When the clock above the blackboard showed eight, the boys he dreaded meeting again strode in ahead of Mrs. Pillow. Behind her came a few boys Wencel recognized from last term.

Mrs. Pillow allowed a few minutes for the boys to settle into their desks and get their books out.

"Welcome to the new spring term, boys. I see familiar faces and I see new ones. This is Pop History Two. Have you all taken Pop History One?" Every hand went up. "Good, good. Let me ask this question ... about the Age of Nerds, which I think we covered last term. What did a typical *nerd* of that period actually look like?"

Wencel's was the first hand to go up. "They wore tight pants, short-sleeved shirts and very thick eye pieces tied around the head with rubber straps."

"Thank you, Wencel ... anyone else?"

Bubba, Penta and Day all raised their hands.

Bubba said, "They had large reproductive organs."

Day said, "Ten times bigger than mine."

"Correct," Mrs. Pillow said, "The size of the average male organ has decreased over time."

Penta said, "The nerds were part smart and part stupid."

"One of them invented the typing machine, a female nerd," said Day. "Her name was Olive Eddie."

"Good answers, boys. You've been doing your homework."

When Mrs. Pillow turned around to chalk something on the blackboard, Bubba, encouraged by Penta and Day, whispered in Wencel's ear, "You're kind of nerd-like, Wency. You got a big organ down there?"

Wencel's face flushed red with anger. He wished these Point Blast boys would leave him alone.

Mrs. Pillow drew a seaside landscape on the board, a beach giving way to an extensive structure of stone and concrete. "Tell me, boys, what is this?"

Gordit, an older student said, "That's the big jetty at Point Blast. The bottomless hole is there."

"Exactly," Mrs. Pillow said. "Now, boys, open your Pop History texts to page 555, *The Presidency of Raymond Gunn*. Who can tell me something about the life of the man who became President Gunn?"

Wencel raised his hand and said, "He was born in a little town called Indian Apple. There was no school there. He grew up in ignorance."

Mrs. Pillow tapped her wooden chalk stick on the rostrum, breaking off its tip. "Anyone else?"

Bubba spoke up again: "Didn't he get kicked in the head by a bugalo?"

"He did," Mrs. Pillow said, "then it was called a *buff*-a-lo."

"What else?"

"He oiled his hair with car grease?"

"Old pictures were said to show that, yes."

"They didn't have the ped back then, did they, Mrs. Pillow? They had motors that moved them around. President Gunn drove a fancy one."

"Yes, boys, and that brings us to motors, the *Age of Motors*. I want you to read that chapter for tomorrow."

The bell rang. It was time for Wencel's next class, General Dramatics. He would have to hustle all the way to the auditorium across the quad, now showing a smattering of spring grass and a few dandelions.

Outside the classroom, Bubba, Penta and Day surrounded him. "Look, Wencel the Pencil, we need a place to stay. Can you find some room at your house or not?"

"There's not an inch of room, I'm sorry."

Bubba reached up and placed his hands loosely around Wencel's neck. "Housing is in short supply, Pencil brain. They bring us here from the Point 'cause our school gets blown up and they don't give us a place to live. We get nothing to eat."

Day said, "Back off, Bubba.... All right, Wencel, you'll have to find a way to make room. We'll be out there for a visit."

Bubba took his hands away from Wencel's neck and the three boys slouched off, mumbling.

Wencel hurried to General Dramatics.

★

Daisy and Wencel's mother finished their shopping with a stop at Annie's Sweet Shop. Annie had just made a batch of licorice drops and the scent of anise oil lingered in the air.

Daisy said, "Give us a bag full."

Annie smiled sweetly. "A whole bag?"

"Just a handful," Wencel's mother said.

Annie poured a handful of drops into a drawstring bag.

Daisy put one of them in her mouth before leaving. "I don't think I have the gene or anything. I like these drops, that's all."

On the ped ride home, Wencel's mother looked closely at Daisy's face for signs that the gene might be expressing. In the beginning there was always a drying and flaking of facial skin above the eyes and a slight pruning of soft flesh under them. She saw none of this, only a clear, healthy-looking complexion.

When they arrived at the stop for the house they were quite surprised to see first a wheeled cart, its bed half filled with rough stones and bags of mortar, then a stone mason finishing his work on a bridge across the ditch, mortaring and placing the last stone. He wore dungarees and a dirty white frock. "You people live here?"

"We do."

"The mortar won't be dry till morning."

He helped Wencel's mother and her trolley over the ditch.

Daisy jumped across.

The mason stood from a crouch, trowel in hand. "Here's your new bridge, ma'am. I'm going from place to place building them. Nobody told me to. I like doing it."

Wencel's mother was aghast. "At least come in for a cup of gadafi and a glass of bitter weed wine."

"Yes, ma'am, love to."

Daisy opened the little bag of drops. "Here, have one of these. You've been working hard."

The mason dipped two mortar-caked fingers into the bag and dragged out a drop. "Thanks, girl, I love these."

Wencel's mother unlocked the front door. "Come on in."

The mason removed his muddy shoes and frock. For a moment, until he pulled down the coarse sweater he was wearing underneath, his thickly-muscled chest was open to the air. Wencel's mother turned away from the sight. She was both pleased by the lovely carpet of hair that covered it nipple to nipple to navel and embarrassed by having seen it.

She unpacked the trolley while Daisy lit the brazier and pumped a bucket of water. "I'll make some gadafi."

Wencel's mother peeled the seal from one of the bottles of bitter weed wine.

"My name's Howard," the mason said. His voice was deep and hoarse, his lower arms thicker than Wencel's legs.

Wencel's mother said, "Howard, have a glass of our bitter wine. It's very strong."

"Yes ma'am, that would be fine, I like wine."

She sat down next to Howard and touched his glass in a toast. "Here's to the new bridge."

Howard said, "Glad to do it. It's a hobby of mine. I build these bridges. It gives me great pleasure."

The toast was carried out with Wencel's mother tilting her glass a bit too far and spilling a few drops on the back of Howard's hand. "Oh, my," she said, "let me get a rag."

Daisy handed her one. She slowly wiped the splat of wine from Howard's hand, with many more easy circular wipes than necessary.

Howard's lush eyebrows arched upward. "Thank you, Mrs. … Miss? What's your name?"

"I don't remember. I lost it all in that big forgetting. My gene blasted husband thought his name was Jimmy, so call me Jane."

Howard said, "Yeah, all I had left was my first name and how to lay one stone on top of another."

Had Wencel been there at that moment, he would have said something like, "I've studied all the Great Forgettings. The first one happened when Michael Ratt was president. No one knew what brought it on, or the others. We still don't."

Wencel's mother lifted the bottle of wine. "Another glass, Howard?"

He placed his hand over the glass. "Oh no, ma'am, I've got to get on down the road with my rig. There's bridges to build over in Pisstown."

"We've got some nice trotters from the souk," Daisy said. "You can stay for dinner. Wencel should be home soon. He's nice."

"That's my son," Wencel's mother said. "You should stay and meet him."

"We're going to have a baby," Daisy said. "We might mate tonight."

"It'll be my grandchild," Wencel's mother said.

Daisy put the trotters on to boil in one pot and the white beans in another. "We have sauce, too."

Wencel's mother playfully brushed the hair on the back of Howard's hand with her fingernails. "Don't rush off. Have dinner with us." She lifted the heavy hand from the wine glass. "And have another wine."

"Yes, ma'am. I've always got a yen for trotters."

She poured him another glass. "Why don't you sleep here and go build your bridges in the morning. After dinner we'll take a walk. The comet is brilliant tonight."

*

It was a little after nine when Wencel got to the auditorium. The three boys from Point Blast had delayed him. He was afraid Professor Flattering, or his replacement, would be angry. If the rumors were to be believed, Flattering could be dead enough to bury. There were other boys, about ten, seated in folding chairs, but no professor. In a way Wencel was relieved he wouldn't be docked for being tardy and wondered at the same time who would be teaching the class. The boys dithered as they waited, some of them talking to others, others simply staring ahead and drumming their fingers against their front teeth or the sides of their heads.

Before Flattering entered the auditorium, the sound of a foot dragging and the *tap-tap* of a walking cane in the hallway could be heard. Wencel stood up and removed his school cap. "I think that's Professor Flattering." The rest of the boys followed suit.

Flattering shuffled in and stood behind the rostrum, leaning on the cane. He seemed decades older than when Wencel had seen him last. His uniform fit him loosely. The whites of his eyes had turned yellow. There was a pronounced hump to his back, forcing his head to bow. The thin, light manuscripts he held in one hand seemed almost too heavy for him to carry.

"Sit down, boys. As you can see, I've taken ill over the holidays. I'm here nevertheless and we're going to have class today. There's some bad news ... the new administration, which is unfriendly to religious displays, has canceled the pageant. But there's good news ... they *will* allow us to put on a play in this very auditorium around the middle of May. I've written it myself. It's called, *The Death of Raymond Gunn*. We start casting today.... Someone come up here and pass out these handwritten manuscripts."

Rogger volunteered and gave one to each boy. Wencel turned to the first page. He was hoping to play one of the parts. It would be a nice departure from his humdrum life at school and his uncertain, befuddling one at home.

Freddy said, "But, sir. We can't read this."

Wencel's hope faded. The scrawl was indeed completely illegible, an up and down saw tooth of a scribble across all the pages top to bottom. There were no indications of character names, or dialog or stage directions.

"Freddy's right, sir. I can't read this either."

"Do your best, boys. I have a mild tremor of the hand. I'm sure you can make out the text if you look hard enough.... If you can't, then be extemporaneous, be impromptu, ad lib.... Who wants to play Raymond Gunn? It's a challenging role to be sure."

Several boys raised their hands, including Wencel.

"We need someone tall, like Wencel," Flattering said.

Wencel produced a strained smile. "They call me The Pencil."

"You'll play Gunn then. Read about his life before you tackle the script."

"I know a lot about him already, sir. We studied him in Pop History. His ascendancy to the presidency can be traced to the Age of Nerds, late period."

"Good, good. That's right. Now, the first casting problem we have is, Gunn had a faithful wife named Flora. And there's Conchita, the president's nurse when he was dying."

Wencel said, "Sir, only two girls were enrolled here. One has gone off to Point Blast and the other one is trying to be a mother. I doubt either one will be back."

"In that case we'll dress up a few of you like females. It's one of the great traditions of dramatic art."

*

Rosy and Jimmy Junior arrived at the Point Blast ped terminal in the middle of the night, the only two passengers. A thick fog rolled in from the water and enveloped the entire Point. Seeing more than an arm's length ahead was impossible. There were electric bulbs on a wire leading down to the beach along an old crumbled stone stairway. Some bulbs were lit, most not, so walking any distance was risky. A misstep could lead to a sprained ankle, a skinned knee, a cracked skull or broken teeth.

The terminal was a tin-roofed pole building without walls, open to the cool, moist night air.

Rosy said, "We should stay here and wait for morning. We'll get lost in the fog."

They got as far away as they could from the noise of the ped's shifting gears and slapping belts and lay on the stone floor.

"Good night, Jimmy Junior."

"Good night, Rosy." Jimmy Junior shivered, gritted his teeth and looked up at the tin roof, wide awake. He knew that Velikovsky was above in the sky, hidden by the roof. He saw it, though; its warm, energetic glow in his mind's dying eye.

Rosy tightened the buttons of her jacket and lay on her back, her hands clasped behind her head as a pillow. She'd learned in Pop History at St. Dymphna's that the ability to dream was lost after the Blast by those with bad genes. She dreamed intermittently as she snatched small periods of sleep. The dream was choppy and indistinct, too abstract to describe to anyone, and wouldn't be remembered.

What woke her at dawn was the sound of waves breaking on sand and the sting of tiny biting flies. She brushed them away from her face and sat up. The fog had lifted and the sun cast a yellow light on things. She scraped the sleep from her eyelids with a fingernail then opened them. She saw a black poodle sitting on its haunches licking Jimmy Junior's dry face.

Jimmy Junior said, "It got off the ped an hour ago. I think it's Fleadle, my father's dog."

"No, Rosy said, "that's not Fleadle.... It looks like Fleadle, but it can't be Fleadle. "

"Whether or not it is Fleadle, it wants to stay with us. It can help me."

"It's very thin. It's been traveling. We'll have to feed it."

"I hear the Point is lousy with rats. It can roam around and comb the beaches for them."

Rosy stood up, shaded her eyes and looked toward the jetty jutting from the shore and encircling a thought-to-be-bottomless lagoon five miles across. The rough stones were faced with a smooth slab of concrete to allow visitors to walk around it. "Oh, look, Jimmy Junior," she said, "let's go down to the Blast site." She helped him to his feet and, along with a few passengers getting off the ped, they walked toward the site, the poodle trotting ahead of them.

"That's Fleadle," Jimmy Junior said. "I'm sure of it. It looked after my father. Now it wants to look after me."

One of the passengers said to Rosy, "They tell me there's no bottom to that lagoon. And that jetty walk around the Blast site is about five miles long."

Jimmy Junior said, "Nobody's really sure when it happened, the Blast, are they?"

The passenger said, "Good lord, young man. I don't care about that. You smell awful. If I were you I'd get that little lady to give me a good shellacking." He stepped up his pace to get some distance from Jimmy Junior.

A female passenger, pinching her nostrils, stepped up to him and said, "That was mean of him. I understand what's happening to you. I had a son with the gene. We had to bury him when he was twenty or thirty or so. I don't remember."

"Thank you, ma'am."

Rosy said, "He smells sweet to me."

It was a steep descent from the ped terminal to the site. In order to keep from falling in the sand and sliding to the bottom, one had to dig one's heels in and lean back. No one wanted to pitch forward and have their face sanded all the way down.

Rosy stood behind Jimmy Junior with a light grip on his shoulders, trying to keep him at the right attitude as they went down the embankment. When they reached bottom they were greeted by beachfront vendors. One blew a little horn between shouts: "Fish patties here.... Get your fish patties." On the brazier, alongside the cooking patties, was a pot of boiling gadafi.

Rosy was hungry. "Let's stop here and get a bite."

"Whatever you want, Rosy girl."

She ordered two patties and a cup of gadafi.

There were rusty metal tables under a shady *palapa*. They chose one and sat there while Rosy had breakfast. Other blast-site visitors sat at nearby tables enjoying the view of the jetty and the beautiful lagoon within its arms, all of them fanning sand flies from their heads and faces.

Rosy asked someone nearby, "Where are the empty cabins? We heard people could live in them."

The woman said, "You can't see them from here. They're right over those dunes. It's quite a tough climb. You keep sliding and sliding."

One of her male companions said, "There're other good reasons them cabins are empty. One thing, they're infested with sand rats. Another thing, the roofs leak and there're no windows. When the wind dies at night, some kind of terrible biting flies swarm in and feed on your blood. Then, some nights a storm blows so much sand in there you wake up under a blanket of it."

The poodle sat near Jimmy Junior, panting, scratching its cheek, its black coat caked with sand.

The woman said, "I hope your poor guy there can make it up that dune."

Rosy drank the last of her gadafi and stood as tall as she could. "I'll carry him if he can't."

The poodle snorted, yawned, and walked languidly toward the foot of the dune, looking back to make sure Rosy, with Jimmy Junior on her back, was in step behind.

*

With spring evident all around him and the setting sun dimming the comet's light, Wencel rode the ped home that evening under a cloudless sky. When he stepped from the ped and saw the new bridge he thought he'd gotten off at the wrong house, possibly the wrong township. He turned to get back on the ped, but hesitated. The house on the other side of the ditch certainly looked like his. The surroundings were familiar. Through the window he could see people seated in the dinette: his mother, Daisy, and a husky male he didn't recognize.

He crossed over the bridge and went into the house.

"There he is," his mother said. "Wencel, this is Howard. He built that bridge. It's hard to believe."

Wencel sat on a wooden bench near the door, took off his school shoes. "Glad to meet you. That's a nice bridge."

Daisy said, "He's having trotters with us. We got them at the souk today."

Wencel's mother placed her hand on the bridge builder's arm and winked. "He'll be staying the night."

Daisy began serving hot trotters in natural gravy. "We've talked it over," she said. "He'll sleep with your mother. I'll sleep with you and show you how to try for a baby."

Wencel's brain blocked up. He had been feeling positive about playing Raymond Gunn in Professor Flattering's play. Now he had no feelings at all other than hunger. He tucked anxiously into his trotters.

Daisy said, "Have some wine, Wencel. It'll relax you."

"I'm fine."

Howard bit into a hot trotter. "Your mother tells me they call you Wencel the Pencil."

"They do."

Howard laughed. "It looks like somebody took you by the feet and pulled you out of your mother too fast."

"I don't remember," Wencel's mother said.

Wencel licked trotter gravy from his lips and wiped the rest away with the back of his hand. "I'm going to be in a play, Mother. I'll be Raymond Gunn, one of the old presidents. Too bad Daisy quit school. She'd be perfect for the young Mrs. Gunn."

"Really? You think I could play the part?"

"I'm sure Professor Flattering would give it to you. Who else?" He handed her his well-fingered script. "It's hard to read."

Howard said, "Who's Raymond Gunn?"

Wencel was annoyed. "I just said he was one of the old presidents."

"I guess I don't remember," Howard said. "I've been through, what, at least three forgettings for gosh sakes?"

"That's why we put on plays. They help people remember what it was like before the Blast."

Daisy turned the pages of Flattering's script. "It's more than hard to read, Wencel. Crooked lines is all it is."

"He said we could make things up, write our own parts, fill in the lines. He's too sick to do it himself. He wants us to do it."

"This is all very interesting," Daisy said. "It sounds like great fun."

Daisy and Wencel sat together for hours that night, filling in the lines of the script with their spoken words and sketching in a few other characters, subject to Flattering's approval. The two were so quickly and tightly focused on their fruitful collaboration, they failed to notice Howard and Wencel's mother tiptoeing down the hall and into her bedroom.

*

When the comet's first light, brightest at dawn, shone through the window of the dinette, Daisy and Wencel were still at work on the script. There were six characters in all. Boys in the class could play the other four. Although Gunn's life was a long and eventful one, the play had to be relatively short, no more than an hour.

"I think we've got a working script," Wencel said.

"I'm going back to school," Daisy said. "I want to be in this play."

"That's clear thinking, Daisy."

"Anyway, it was your mother's idea for us to mate and have her grandchild. It never seemed right. I'm not doing it."

Wencel said, "We're too young to mate. I'm scared to try."

Wencel knew from his study of Pop History that just before the period of depopulation, a great forgetting occurred. Sexually mature males and females alike emerged from it with a severely diminished urge to mate. The "congressional act" as it was called then, was rarely performed, accounting for the currently sparse population, living in townships scattered haphazardly here and there, often many miles apart.

Daisy gave Wencel a little peck on the cheek. "I've got to get ready for school."

Wencel's mother tiptoed down the hall into the dinette wearing only socks and under-drawers, with a towel wrapped over her shoulders covering her small breasts. One of her eyes was bruised, there were abrasions on her face and her nose bled. She wiped the blood with a tea towel.

Wencel turned away. "What happened, Mother?"

"Howard and I mated last night. He'll be living here now and we won't have room for a child. He's a rough man, he hurt me in every way, but we're in love."

Daisy said, "That's perfect. I'm *not* mating with Wencel. I'm going back to school to be in a play."

Wencel's mother pumped water for gadafi and lit the brazier, saying nothing more.

All could hear Howard's rough snoring as it echoed in the hall.

*

Rosy carried Jimmy Junior on her back up the steep dune. Fleadle walked alongside her, always looking up to make sure she was holding him tight enough. If not, Rosy would get a nip on the leg. At the top of the dune, with her ankles pricked by needle grass and poodle nips, and bleeding, she set Jimmy Junior down. Fleadle licked his dangling hand.

There were abandoned cabins everywhere they looked. Some were ramshackle, with collapsed roofs and broken windows. The first one that appeared reasonably livable from the outside was infested inside with spiders and the wallpaper stained with black mildew. The second one they explored was near the dune's edge and offered an outdoor privy, a clear view of the Point, the lagoon, and the jetty. It would be in the path of evening breezes from the water, which would keep the biting bugs at bay.

Jimmy Junior said, "What could be better? This is where I'll live out my days."

The cabin steps sagged but didn't break when they climbed them. A rusted screen and the sand-blasted door behind it stood open. Rosy loved the wooden floors, working windows, the kitchen's sink, and a pump that brought water after just a few tries. Off the main room was a small bedroom with a dirty mattress on the floor. There were no furnishings to be seen other than a wooden rocking chair and a sand-soaked sofa missing two of its three pillows. In the kitchen Rosy found a few pots and pans, metal plates, a sack of coals for the brazier, some matches, a few knives and forks.

Jimmy Junior sat in the rocking chair but was too weak and too fatigued to rock. He sat still, tried to catch his breath and savored the view from the front window. There were new arrivals having a walking tour of the jetty. At the far curve a cluster of people fished. Beyond that the water was as blue as the sky.

Rosy found an old straw broom leaning against the back door. She swept sand from the cottage until her arms ached, then sat on the sofa facing Jimmy Junior. "We can live here, Jimmy Junior. We need food and a few other things, but we can live here. In the morning I'll go around and see what I can find in the empty cabins. Maybe a futon, maybe a candle. Who knows?"

"Be careful," Jimmy Junior said. "Knock first. We're not the only ones here." He sat up all night in the rocking chair. He could hear the distant, faint sound of waves breaking on the jetty. Rosy fell asleep sitting up on the sofa's gritty cushion. The poodle slept on the floor by the rocking chair, its stomach growling with hunger. Hours later, when the night breeze stopped, biting flies blew in the open door and windows and feasted on Rosy the rest of the night. Jimmy Junior, unable to feel the bites, and the poodle, with thickly curled hair, were not bothered by the swarm.

When Rosy awoke shortly before dawn, Jimmy Junior said, "The comet is beautiful this morning. Let's go out and look. I want to feel the sea air. It's so fresh at sunup."

Rosy rubbed her eyes, scratched her bites, tried to organize her tousled red hair with her fingertips, then helped Jimmy Junior down the front steps and into the yard's mix of sand and needle grass. The poodle ran off, skirting the crest of the dune, looking for rats. Rosy and Jimmy Junior sat in the sand and marveled at the twinkle of the comet's tail.

Rosy had to empty her bowels. She walked behind the cottage to the privy. Even within a few feet of the little building she heard grunting and tugged at the door. It was locked from the inside.

"Hold on there. I'll be done in a minute." The voice came from an older man.

"I'm sorry, I didn't expect to find anyone in there."

Rosy backed away to a safe distance from the sound of dropping turds until the door opened and a weather-worn man in dungarees stepped out.

"Sorry, lady. We all use this one. It's the best around. You got a good cottage there. People moved out only about ten years ago. It's in good condition."

"We like it. We need food, though."

"Go on down the dune a ways. There's an old army road. They built it before the Blast. Step around that rusty gate and follow the road about a mile. There's a store there, the only one we've got. The people that run it are awful people, hateful and mean. Sometimes I wish they'd kill one another. We need a new store right here at the edge of the dune."

"My name is Rosy. I'm staying with a friend who has bad genes. He's Jimmy Junior. I guess it's a second generation thing. He got it from his father. Where do you live?"

"Pretty close, a few cottages over that way. I'm Stanley Gunn. Me and my wife stay there. She's got the gene, too. This is where she wanted to be, near the water, near the Point."

"Most of them want to come here at the end," Rosy said. "I don't know why."

"Don't you think it must be like going home again, like returning to your birthplace? This is where it all started for them, the big Blast, the gene shower. So it's a good place to finish."

"That sounds right, Mr. Gunn. Thank you for those directions. I'm off to the store. We need lots of things."

"Bring your friend over sometime. Him and my wife can commiserate."

"We'll come over when we get settled."

"That's a nice poodle you got."

"He's an angel. His name is Fleadle."

*

Daisy and Wencel walked freely onto the campus of St. Cuth's that morning a few minutes before eight. All six spigots of the fountain spurted at full strength. The weather was warm and clear, though rain clouds loomed in the south.

Wencel said, "We were supposed to read about the Age of Motors. We didn't get around to it. We were up all night with the play."

"I know about the Age of Motors. We learned that at St. Dymphna's."

"Good, Daisy, that's good."

Wencel saw the three boys from Point Blast sitting in the back row, looking at him with slanted smiles. He quickly sat down and faced forward.

Mrs. Pillow began the class by holding up a drawing. "I sketched this myself. It represents what I think a motor looked like." The sketch showed an elongate tube made of a shiny material speeding down a road of black mud. The vehicle seemed to be propelled by spinning disks beneath its belly and expelled smoke or steam from the rear. "Tell me, class, what brought an end to the Age of Motors?"

Daisy was the first to raise her hand. "The motors stopped running."

"Why?"

Bubba said, "They ran out of gas."

"Yes," Mrs. Pillow said. "They ran out of gas. What then? How did people get from place to place?"

No one seemed to know, but there were no shortage of guesses.

"They walked?"

"Didn't they have flying motors? Like the one you drew, except in the sky?"

Mrs. Pillow shook her head. "No, no. Without gas, they fell to the ground."

"They made trains?"

"Yes," Mrs. Pillow said, "they made trains that ran on boiled water.... And that led to what?"

"They burned up almost all the trees to boil the water."

"Correct.... And that led to?"

"The invention of the pedway," Wencel said.

Mrs. Pillow clapped her hands. "Exactly! Now tell me who invented the ped?"

"A man named Stanley Gunn," Wencel said, "great grandson of President Gunn."

"It was, Wencel, as far as we know. What we don't know is what became of Stanley Gunn. He's been lost to history."

*

After Wencel and Daisy left for school, Wencel's mother served Howard a stack of johnny cakes. "Gadafi?"

"Yeah."

It had begun to rain, a hard shower passing through from the south.

"The ditch will flood if this keeps up," Howard said. He went to the window. The ditch had risen a foot already and the black clouds were so dense the comet was a dim bulb behind them. "The bridge'll hold. No doubt about that." He saw three boys get off the ped and run through the mud to the house. One of them knocked.

It startled Wencel's mother. "Is that Wencel and Daisy?"

"It's some boys from the school."

"Let them in. They must be friends of Wencel's."

"They look like trouble." Howard slammed one fist into the palm of the other hand.

"Don't be silly, Howard. Let them in."

Howard opened the door. Penta, Bubba and Day stepped inside, dripping water and tracking mud.

"Where's Wencel," his mother wanted to know.

Day said, "He and that girl went to General Dramatics class. They're putting on a play."

Penta said, "We don't take that class. It's stupid and the teacher looks like a mummy."

Day said, "The thing is, Wencel said we could stay here a few nights. We came up from Point Blast to go to St. Cuth's but there's no place to stay. We'll sleep on the floor if we have to. He said you would feed us, too, just for a few days. We're going back to the Point pretty soon, maybe in a week. We hate it here."

Bubba said, "We're hungry as dirt right now."

Wencel's mother said, "I'm sorry. We don't have any room."

"Wencel said you did."

The three boys sat at the dinette table. Day said, "What's that I smell? Johnny cakes. I'd love some."

Wencel's mother shrugged. She didn't know what to do. The boys had dripped water and tracked mud in a trail from the door to the table, something Wencel would never consider doing. These couldn't be his friends and he couldn't have told them they could stay here. She looked at Howard and waved a hooked thumb toward the front door. She wanted them out of her house. She wouldn't be making them any johnny cakes.

Howard said, "Get out and get back on that ped."

Penta said, "We'd rather stay here."

Howard said, "You boys better step on that ped and get to the Point. Can't you see that black sky in the middle of the day? There's a flood coming." He stepped toward them and raised his fist. "Go on, now."

Wencel's mother said, "You should go, boys. He'll hurt you."

Penta and Day scuttled toward the door, leaving a second trail. Bubba stood and faced Howard straight on. "Who are you, Mister Puffgut, to tell us we can't stay here after Wencel said we could?"

"He never said that," Wencel's mother said. "Howard, get those liars out of my house."

Howard struck Bubba with a violent blow to the face, driving him backward against the brazier, raking his back with hot coals as he fell and setting his school jacket on fire. As rain-damp as it was, the flames were out in a moment. Howard then went around the dinette and kicked Bubba in the ribs with his heavy mason's boot. Bubba rolled over and groaned, the back of his jacket steaming. Howard picked up his feet and dragged him to the door. To Penta and Day he said, "Take your friend and get on down the road."

Both Howard and Wencel's mother watched from the window as they helped the stumbling Bubba onto the ped.

"They're nothing like Wencel," Wencel's mother said.

*

As Rosy walked down the army road, the sandy soil gave way to hard-packed gravel and passed through a patch of bitter weed into an open field of old motors. She had seen drawings of them in one of her texts at St. Dymphna's. Here they were lined up side by side, hundreds of them, all rusted, the green paint peeling in the salty sea air. She realized they must have been there since the time of the Blast, their drivers either dead or gone.

Beyond the field was the store, a metal building with a rounded roof. Someone had painted a sign on its side saying simply STORE. Behind it, only a few yards away, stood a cottage with a small porch and a swing. In the swing sat a man and a woman of middle age, who appeared to be arguing. Lying at the other end of the porch was a white poodle baring its teeth.

The man stood. "Come on over here, girl. We're open day and night."

"We are not!" The woman shouted. "We are *not* open at night. Don't listen to what that idiot says."

"Close that mouth and stop harping at me! What do you need, girl?"

The poodle ran ahead and sniffed Rosy's feet.

"We moved into a cottage back there close to the water, a friend and I. We need to get some food. What do you have?"

The woman headed toward the back of the store. "Go on around to the front and go in. We'll go in the back."

The man said, "We have a lot of food, even licorice drops for your friend."

The woman countered, "We have *some* food, not a lot, and we definitely don't have any licorice drops."

"What about shellac and brushes? Do you have those?"

"No, none of that, nothing like that," the woman said. "We used to carry them. We don't any more. Not much demand. Old man Gunn shellacked his wife years ago, but that's all till you."

Rosy said, "I'll go in and see what's there. Almost anything will help. My friend's got the bad gene and doesn't eat, but I'm very hungry. I'm hoping our poodle can go out and find rats to eat."

She entered the building expecting to see the man and woman meet her. But the back door was closed. Assuming they had been delayed by something or other, or had to go back to the cottage to get a key perhaps, she looked around the store to see what food there was.

There were pull-down bins along the length of one wall, most of them empty. She did find three that were not. In one was corn meal, in another flour, and in the third a good supply of what was labeled dry pizzles. There were burlap bags hanging from a nail. She helped herself to flour and corn meal for johnny cakes and pizzles to go with them. She had seen fresh pizzles for sale once at the souk. These she would have to boil a long time.

She found oil to make the johnny cakes and fry the pizzles once they were fleshed out, but unfortunately there was only a small sack of gadafi powder. Otherwise she had what she needed and most of what was available. It was a long walk back. They were to meet her. It was late afternoon. She had seen them at the back door ready to enter. Where were they? She didn't want to be going back down that army road after dark. And she'd left Jimmy Junior at the cottage to make do. It was a good thing he didn't need to eat, drink or use the privy.

She went to the back door and opened it. Outside stood Stanley Gunn, who said, "I'm sorry I sent you here. The people who run this place were so rotten to the core I couldn't stand it."

"Where are they?"

"In the cottage. I saw them through the screen door, dead on the couch. I went in. It looked like they had stabbed one another with the same knife if you can believe that. I don't know how many times I told those idiots to close it down and move it closer to the Point. There's not a lot of us there, but there's nobody here. We need a real store, like a little souk. It's stupid walking all the way out here and they've got almost nothing in stock. Come on, I'll walk you back."

"Should we leave the bodies there?"

"They can just rot as far as I'm concerned."

The thought disturbed Rosy a bit, but she was happy to have what she had. For now, there was no store at the Point. There were vendors down along the beach if you were willing to slide down the side of the dune and get your bottom stuck with needle grass and your face slapped by bitter weed, then slip and slide your way up again, an exhausting venture.

It was a leisurely walk back for Gunn and Rosy. He helped her with her sacks. There was a bit of a gimp in one of his legs and he walked slowly and unevenly.

"Mr. Gunn, I do appreciate you helping me. You can use my privy any time."

"My wife uses it too. You haven't met Mrs. Gunn."

"No, I haven't."

"She's quite the cook. Her trotters are divine. You and your friend will be coming over for dinner very soon."

"He doesn't eat, but I do."

"That's fine. We'll sit him on the porch and he can look out at the water."

"You're nice, Mr. Gunn."

"You can call me Stan."

"Stan Gunn ... forgive me, but we studied about Raymond Gunn at St. Dymphna's. There aren't that many Gunns around today. Are you descended from him?"

Gunn hacked up a bit of phlegm and spat it into the dirt. "My granddaddy."

"So you're the Stanley Gunn who invented the ped."

"I am."

"They said in school you were lost to history."

"Lost, forgotten, hidden. It doesn't matter. And I didn't really *invent* the ped. I *designed* the ped. I *engineered* the ped. I worked out the *route* of the ped. I figured out how to make it *waterproof*."

By then they were passing the field of motors. Rosy said, "We learned about the Blast, too."

"Not much to learn," Gunn said. "Everybody forgot. It's lost to history, like me."

Just before reaching the rusty gate that led out of the army road, Gunn said, "If you look over yonder there you can see what's left of St. Gilbert's. It was a school for boys. It blew up and all the boys who weren't killed left for the townships."

All Rosy could see was a pile of bricks and stone and a standing chimney scorched black.

"I heard about that on the radio," she said.

Mr. Gunn stopped walking for a moment. "You have a radio?"

"Not any more. I left it back in Outerditch."

"Too bad. We had one but the crank broke. That's all right, though. We like it here and we've got no interest knowing what goes on in the townships."

When they reached Rosy's cottage, Rosy said, "Thank you for helping me, Mr. Gunn."

"Good night, Rosy. It's best to soak dry pizzles overnight before you boil them."

Rosy said, "I do hope we get a store here. And I hope it'll have licorice drops."

"We will, we will. I have connections in Bunkerville. We can get them sent in on the ped."

Rosy wasn't surprised to hear about the storekeepers killing one another. She had read that when the Point re-opened to the public for the first time after the Blast and all the old cabins became available, a number of the early occupiers were antagonists, fighting over one thing and another. Manslaughter and outright killings were fairly common, even among husbands and wives. The victims were buried, burned or left in fields to rot, soon forgotten.

*

Wencel and Daisy took their seats in the auditorium and waited for Professor Flattering. There was a buzz among the other students about the weather.

"I heard it on my radio," one of them said. "It's going to rain all day every day for at least a week, maybe a month."

Wencel ran to the window. The rain came down in a torrent. Drops falling and striking the pavement were as large as he had ever seen. Professor Flattering, in a raincoat and hat, made his way toward the auditorium from across the quad. The wind picked up and gusted, blowing him both sideward and backward, so that he wasn't making any progress.

"We should go out there and help him," Wencel said, but made no move to do that.

Nor did any of the boys.

Daisy stood up. "I'll go get him."

The boys watched as she ran out of the auditorium and half way across the quad, trying to catch Flattering, who was being blown out of her reach by gusts of wind. Eventually she caught hold of a corner of his raincoat and pulled him down. She held on to his feet to keep him from blowing any further. Already an inch or two of water flowed across the quad, also pulling at Flattering's light, buoyant body.

"Let me go, dear," he said with a dramatic flair, "let the water take me. I'm finished and so is the play."

The rain fell so hard it stung Daisy's head. Water rushed against her ankles. She let Flattering go and splashed through deepening water to the auditorium. Wencel and the other boys were gathered at the windows watching Flattering float away toward the now-flooded fountain.

Daisy shouted through the window, "Wencel! Let's get on the ped before it stops in all that water."

Wencel knew the ped wouldn't stop. It had been running for ages, sometimes slowing, sometimes speeding up, but never stopping. Mrs. Pillow had said that in Pop History.

The rain fell heavier than ever, the sky black, the water above Daisy's ankles. Mrs. Pillow was nowhere in sight. Wencel and the other boys poured out of the auditorium onto the quad, now a shallow but wide river, and all ran for the ped.

Howard wondered if his bridge might give way. Another foot of water could undermine it, his cart could wash away and all his tools would be lost. "I'm going out. I have to get my tools and have a look at the bridge."

Wencel's mother folded her arms and shook her head. "I'm scared for Daisy and Wencel. I hope the ped doesn't stop running."

"Hell, it's running. I can hear it even under the water."

The stress of the situation jogged Wencel's mother's recent memory. "You know what I forgot? That crank radio Rosy left. It's in the closet. They'll say something about the weather."

"Go get it then. Crank it and listen to it. I'm going out."

An inch of water rushed into the entryway before Wencel's mother could close the door behind Howard. She went to the little window in the kitchenette to see what he was doing. Rain pounded against the pane so hard that she backed away, fearing it would break and the glass would cut her.

She found the radio in the closet, sat down in the kitchenette and cranked it until her arms hurt then turned the needle across the dial, beginning to end. The only signal strong enough to hear was a weather report out of Bunkerville. Conditions were sketchy for most of the townships, particularly Pisstown's lowlands, reported to be all but under water. At Point Blast the weather was fair and mild with clear skies and not a hint of rain.

Howard managed to anchor his cart by placing stones under its wheels, and made his way to the bridge against the current. There was some erosion of the ditch bank around the footing. That would be a worry if the rain kept up, and there was no promise it would stop any time soon. The bridge could collapse into the ditch. There was nothing to do about it now. He turned to go back to the house until he heard Wencel's voice coming from the ped. "Howard, tell Mother we're going to the Point."

As he and Daisy passed by, waving, Daisy said, "The teacher's dead, the play is canceled."

"And the school is flooded," Wencel added.

As they moved farther on, it was difficult for Howard to hear them against the sound of pelting rain. The last thing he could make out was Wencel shouting, "Come to the Point as soon as you can."

Howard returned to the house and went in. There was water ankle deep all over the house and cascading into the cellar. Wencel's mother sat on the dinette table cranking the radio.

"There's clear skies at the Point. People are going there. Cottages are getting scarce."

"Maybe so. Your boy and Daisy went by on the ped. They're going there. They said we should go, too. That's what they said."

Wencel's mother held the radio to her ear and listened. The signal from Bunkerville was gone. She twisted the dial to see if another township might be broadcasting. A weak signal from flooded Pisstown came in. Wencel's mother could hear it just well enough to know that residents there were being advised to get on the ped and go to the Point. "Let's go now," she said.

*

When Rosy returned to the cottage, she found Jimmy Junior sitting on the porch watching Fleadle chase rats, kill some, catch others and play with them, then let them go.

Jimmy Junior said, "That poodle is very smart. It leaves some of them alive to assure a good supply of rats going forward. And, a few hours after rotting in the sun, the rest are ready to eat. Fleadle has a system."

"I'm tired," Rosy said. "I have a few groceries. I'm going in to soak some pizzles for tomorrow. They didn't have any drops. I'm sorry."

"I don't expect anything and I don't need anything."

"You do smell. You need a shellacking. Maybe the store will have some when it opens. That man who uses our privy, Mr. Gunn, he invented the ped. And he's going to open a store."

"Mrs. Gunn came by while you were gone. She told me all about him. We're invited there for dinner tonight. She said it would be something nice for you, something from the sea. For me she actually has some drops. She's got the gene, too."

"Dinner will be nice," Rosy said. "I'm so tired."

"His wife told me about the store. A store would be nice for Point people who need to eat. For me, it doesn't matter at all."

"The owners of the store down the road killed one another with the same knife. Mr. Gunn saw the bodies."

Jimmy Junior wondered for a moment how that could be done with a single knife. If one of them had first fatally stabbed the other, how could the other use the same knife to return a fatal blow? After running through a series of possible scenarios in his mind, he gave up.

Rosy went inside, pumped up a pot of water and put the pizzles in to soak.

*

As the pedway floor curved into the terminal at Point Blast, it spilled water. Daisy and Wencel stepped off rain-soaked and wind-blown. Other refugees from the flooded townships arrived by twos and threes. Beyond the terminal roof, the comet shone as brightly as the late afternoon sun. Several vendors pushed their carts up to the terminal, offering fish cakes, pizzle jerky and bitter weed juice.

Daisy, wet, shivering and hungry, ordered a jerky and a glass of juice.

Wencel said, "Nothing for me. I feel a little sick."

Daisy asked one of the vendors the way to the empty cabins. He pointed toward the jetty. "Go on down to the beach, turn right, walk a ways till you get to that big dune. Go up that dune and you'll see them. I got to tell you, there's not many left that's worth living in."

"We have relatives here. Maybe you know them ... Rosy Doolittle and Jimmy Junior, her friend. He's got the gene and it's expressing fast. She's a pretty girl. He's a half-gone wreck."

"He's my half-brother, too," Wencel said.

"They have a cottage up there. You'll find them."

Daisy and Wencel walked down to the beach. Following them, probably with the same intentions, were five or six people Daisy recognized from the souk.

She turned to them. "If cottages are so scarce, you can go ahead of us. We have a place to stay."

The group was thankful and galloped off in a small herd.

Daisy finished her jerky and juice and took Wencel's hand. "Let's walk all the way around the jetty."

"That would take hours. It'll be dark."

"Tomorrow, then?"

"All right."

They walked hand in hand until they came to the big dune. Scaling it would take both hands and strong legs. Wencel suggested they make the assault several feet apart rather than one behind the other so as not to kick sand in anyone's face. Daisy agreed and they made their way up, grasping the occasional bitter weed for leverage, hoping not to pull it out of the sand and slide backward into a patch of needle grass. On one slide, without Wencel's notice, six of his father's teeth were shaken out of his uniform pocket into the sand. The seven in his other pocket remained where they were.

Fleadle greeted them at the crest of the dune with a wagging tail, a bow, a yawn and a snort.

"It's Fleadle," Daisy said. She gave the poodle a petting.

Wencel said, "There's a cabin up there with a light in the window. Let's go there. That has to be the place."

Daisy and the poodle were not far behind him.

"I'll be so happy to see my sister," Daisy said.

The poodle took the lead and led them to the steps of the lighted cottage.

Wencel rapped on the screen door. As they waited for someone to answer, the poodle settled down and chewed on a sand rat carcass.

No one answered. But the screen was unlocked. Wencel and Daisy went in. The light they'd seen was coming from glowing coals in the brazier. Daisy lifted the lid of a pot on the counter. "Pizzles," she said. "Rosy loves them. This is where they're staying. I wonder where they are."

"I don't know. They'll come back. Put those pizzles on the brazier. I'm hungry. Rosy won't mind."

"You should've gotten something from the vendors like I did."

"I wasn't hungry right at that moment. Then comes the climb up here. Now I need food. I feel weak. I'm all stuck with needle grass."

"I am, too, Wencel. Stop acting like a baby."

As the pizzles boiled, Daisy and Wencel sat on the sandy sofa, crowded onto the middle cushion. The other two were lying on the floor, rat-gnawed, their springs popping through the upholstery.

Wencel stretched out his long legs and put his hands in his pockets. "I know what we can do while we're waiting." His left hand drew out seven emoticon-marked teeth. His right fished around in the pocket and found nothing. "I've lost some. They must have fallen out. We'll have to play with seven. It's a game I invented with my father's teeth.... Let's sit on the floor and cast them out. You first, Daisy." She held out both hands with open palms. He placed the seven teeth in them. "Cup your hands together now, shake the teeth then throw three of them out on the floor."

Daisy shook and threw the teeth onto the sandy wooden floor. They landed in a tight cluster:

: { = Sad

:' (= Crying

D : < = Horror

"That's not good," Wencel said. "My turn. I'll throw three and save one." Wencel threw the teeth:

>:(= Angry

O: --) = Angel

>;) = Evil

"I don't like that," Daisy said.

"Throw the last tooth." Wencel dropped it into Daisy's sweaty palm. She threw it into the sand:

:') = Tears of Happiness

"It will end well," Wencel said.

There was no sleep for Howard or Wencel's mother that night, most of it spent standing on the dinette table in the dark to stay above the water. The brazier had gone out, the lights too. Every now and then Wencel's mother cranked the radio and listened closely to a barely audible weather report from Bunkerville.

"It's sunny and warm at the Point, Howie. It never rains. Wencel's there, Daisy's there, Rosy's there, Jimmy Junior is there. Why not us? We could get a cottage. We could live there. This house is ruined. Everything important is under water."

"Just leave, you mean, leave the house?"

"Walk out, get on the ped and go."

"Excuse me," Howard said. "Is your name Judy? I forgot."

"Didn't we decide it was Jane? Isn't my name Jane? I forgot, too."

"Oh, Jane, that's right."

"We won't be coming back, Howie. When we leave this house, people will move in, people worse off than us."

In the morning, when the rains ended, Howard went out, wading through knee-deep water, to see that his bridge had fallen over and lay on its side. His cart remained tethered to the ground, but every tool, every stone and every bag of mortar had washed away. His days of building bridges were over. He told himself he was getting too old for strenuous work anyway. Retiring to the Point would be an attractive option.

Aside from the maximine, which had been placed in a high cabinet in the kitchenette, and the radio, everything in the house worth retrieving was either water logged or under water.

"Let's go," Howard said.

They waded to the ped with only the wet clothes they were wearing, a bag of maximine swinging in Wencel's mother's hand, the crank radio tucked under Howard's arm.

Rosy and Jimmy Junior were enjoying dinner at the Gunn's. As promised, Mrs. Gunn served a large fish she'd grilled on the brazier. "It's a drum fish," she said. "Stan caught it yesterday out on the jetty."

Mr. Gunn sat up straight. "You have to go all the way out there. It's a three-mile walk. That's where you catch the drums, in the middle of the Blast hole. I use rat tails for bait and a number five hook."

Rosy said, "It's a very nice fish." She lifted hunks of it onto her plate.

Mrs. Gunn poured glasses of bitter weed wine for everyone but Jimmy Junior. She served him a small plate of licorice drops. "We'll share," she said. "I still like the wine but the drops are all I can stomach."

"So, Mr. Gunn, I hear you invented the ped," Jimmy Junior said.

"That was ages ago, son. I've forgotten all about it."

"He'd rather talk about other things," Mrs. Gunn said.

Jimmy Junior sucked on a licorice drop and asked him what he wanted to talk about.

"He has a confession to make," Mrs. Gunn said. "Go ahead, Stan."

"Those two people at the store I said had killed one another with the same knife. That's not true. I killed them myself. They were miserable people, full of hate. I found a monkey wrench in the barn and clubbed them senseless with it. My apologies for lying. They had to go, though. I'm not apologizing for that. We need a store here, not way over there on the army road."

"As I said," Mrs. Gunn said, "we'll have drops for people like me and Jimmy Junior."

"Killing the wicked can be good sometimes," Rosy said. "They told us that at St. Dymphna's."

"I'm not sure dying is all that bad," Jimmy Junior said. "I feel pretty good."

"I do, too," Mrs. Gunn said. "What's all the fuss?"

Jimmy Junior heaved forward in his chair and coughed up a half-dissolved licorice drop into a napkin. "I'm so sorry."

"Don't worry," Mrs. Gunn said. "It happens to me all the time." She took away the blackened napkin and brought him a fresh one.

"Thank you very much, Mrs. Gunn. I'm glad we were able to get a cabin near yours."

"And meet good people right away," Rosy said. She raised her glass. "To the Gunns."

Mr. Gunn raised his glass and touched it to Rosy's. "To you and your young friend, bad genes and all."

Mrs. Gunn was able to lift her glass in the toast with a strenuous effort. "To the store, the store we're going to build and stock with everything we can get."

Jimmy Junior had no wine and wanted none. Able to raise his arm less than a foot, he clutched an empty glass and said, "Cheers."

Rosy lifted another helping of the drum from its bone to her plate. "This fish is delicious. I can't stop eating it."

Mrs. Gunn poured her another glass of wine. "You can only eat drum in the spring. In the summer they get liver flukes."

Mr. Gunn, tipsy, asked, "Have you two been out on the jetty yet? Come fishing with me, soon."

Jimmy Junior shook his head, resulting in a small shower of dead skin. "I can't walk that far." He sneezed a worm into his napkin. "I'm sorry, Mrs. Gunn. This is the second mess I've made."

"Don't worry at all. I understand."

Rosy said, "I'll go fishing with you, Mr. Gunn. I don't have a pole or any tackle, though."

"Take mine," Mrs. Gunn said. "I haven't used it in ages."

Mr. Gunn's head drooped. "We'll go in the morning, early. Drum bite when the comet's brightest." He nodded off.

Mrs. Gunn stroked her sleeping husband's hair and lost a fingernail in the process. "He'll be down on the beach before dawn." She picked the nail out of his hair, wrapped it in Jimmy Junior's wormy napkin and threw it into the bin. "Meet him at the foot of the jetty. He'll have everything you need."

Jimmy Junior said, "We should be going back to our cabin. It's getting late. I don't sleep but Rosy does."

Rosy stood up. "And it looks like I'm getting up early.... Good night."

Mrs. Gunn held Rosy's hand. "I hope you don't believe he killed those store keepers. I'm sure they killed one another. He followed you out there and made up that story to explain why he was there. You can't depend on anything he says. He *didn't* invent the ped ... he *did* invent the ped. Who knows? I don't know and I'm his wife."

★

Daisy and Wencel heard the screen door open. They assumed it was Rosy and Jimmy Junior coming home. Wencel scooped up the teeth and put them into his pocket. Daisy stood up, preparing to give her sister a hug. Instead, four former St. Cuthbert's students stepped one at a time into the cabin's tiny parlor, sand sliding under their bare feet. Wencel had seen them before: Bubba, Penta, Day and Butch, the gate guard.

"Hey, Wencel the Pencil. We saw you through the window." It was Butch, but with a friendly tone in his voice.

"Hello. Butch."

Bubba said, "That idiot that lives with your mother fucked us up pretty good, you know."

"I didn't know." Wencel was still sitting on the floor. He stood up.

Day said, "It doesn't matter. We're happy down here. Lots of sun. Free cabins. Ours is right down the lane.... Do you mind if we use your privy? Ours is full."

Wencel and Daisy shrugged. They didn't want trouble. "It's not really our privy," Wencel said.

"My sister and her friend live here," Daisy said. "It's their privy."

"But go ahead and use it," Wencel said.

Penta said, "That's fair. All is forgiven. Look, we're going to the beach early tomorrow for a swim. Come on down there and enjoy yourselves. After the swim, we'll take some maximine and grill some sea slugs."

Bubba said, "We only got a little bit of maxi left. You two want one?"

Wencel held out his fist and unfurled his fingers. "I do."

"Sounds like fun," Daisy said.

Bubba gave them each a blue maximine.

"Good night then," Butch said. "We'll see you first thing in the morning."

The four trooped out of the cabin in single file.

Wencel remembered the metamine his mother always gave him when he was ill. It fogged his mind a little, but he felt quite good for a while and then slept deeply. Afterward, he'd forgotten bits and pieces of what he knew, in many ways a relief.

"What are sea slugs?" Daisy asked. "I think I knew but I forgot."

"I forgot too," Wencel said. "I know all about land slugs. I've seen them in the basement. I picked them off my father a few times."

Daisy swallowed her maximine and lay on the sandy floor. "I'm sleepy already. I wonder where Rosy and Jimmy Junior are?"

Wencel swallowed his and lay head-to-toe near her. "I don't know. I'm exhausted."

The maximine let Wencel have a few hours of restful sleep before the comet's light awakened him. This time he thought he heard the sizzle that people were talking about, a sound the comet had begun to make that was like a trotter frying in the pan. Some thought the comet was burning up, though most agreed that a block of flying ice larger than the moon would never catch fire.

Rosy and Jimmy Junior had tiptoed in during the night. Rosy slept in the small bedroom at the rear of the cabin. Jimmy Junior sat up in the rocking chair, wide awake, and in the morning heard Wencel pumping water in the kitchenette, waking Rosy up. She got up from the dingy mattress and greeted Wencel in the kitchenette with a little pat on his shoulder, standing on tiptoe to do so.

"Is there any gadafi?" he asked.

"A little. Let me make a pot of it."

Now Daisy joined them and gave Rosy a sisterly hug and kiss.

Rosy said, "The most interesting people are living around here. We love it." She draped a flannel chemise over Jimmy Junior's shoulders. "I found this in the closet. You look cold."

"We were flooded out," Wencel said. "That's why we came."

Daisy said, "I hope we can stay awhile. We'll sleep on the floor."

Wencel said, "I'll sleep out in the sand with Fleadle. I don't care. I'm happy to be here."

"After we drink our gadafi, let's all go down to the beach," Rosy said. "Some friends are having a little breakfast party and I'm going fishing with Stan Gunn."

"Stan Gunn ... *the* Stan Gun, inventor of the ped?"

"Yes, he lives right down the lane. We were having dinner there last night. His wife's got the gene."

"I like her," Jimmy Junior said. "I sneezed a worm into one of her napkins and she didn't get angry."

"They have a lot in common," Rosy said.

*

Wencel's mother tried to comfort Howard on the way to the Point. His spirit sagged pitiably. He draped himself over the ped's moving rail, hanging his head and shoulders over the side. "What's the use? I'm finished."

"Howie. It'll be wonderful living at the Point. And I'm sure they'll need something you can build."

When they reached the end of the line at the Point Blast Terminal, they were exhausted. The flood had taken everything but the maximine, the radio and the wet clothing they were wearing.

"Let's just stand here and be still for a few minutes," Wencel's mother said. She placed an arm over Howard's shoulder. "This will be our second life. We'll walk our bodies around in a different world here."

"Give me a maxi," Howard said, "before I drown myself."

She gave him two and he swallowed them.

"Let's go find the kids," she said, taking Howard's meaty hand and leading him down to the beach. It was about dawn. Between the comet and the rising sun it was a bright day already. Vendors approached as they neared the jetty.

"I got fried pizzles."

"Get fish cakes over here."

"Bitter weed cola by the glass?"

"I *am* kind of hungry," Howard said.

Wencel's mother gave each of the vendors a maximine and said, "Give him a pizzle, a cake, and a glass of cola. I'll have just a cola."

"Yes, ma'am. One crank." He wrapped the sizzling pizzle in waxed paper. "I see you got a radio. Not too many of them around the Point. You better keep an eye on it."

Another offered a fish cake. "Ma'am...."

"Yes, and two glasses of cola," a third vendor offered.

Howard ate at a bench in the shade of a little straw-roofed *palapa*. Wencel's mother drank her cola and watched four boys work together to light a brazier fire down the beach a ways.

"Look, Howard. We know those boys. They came to the house and you fucked them up."

Howard rubbed his eyes and had a look. "Yeah, that's them, and another one."

One of the boys chopped away at sea slugs on a driftwood log while the others fanned the brazier with their shirts.

Butch noticed Howard looking at them and alerted the others by tapping their shoulders. "Who's that yonder who's so interested in us, those people under the *palapa*?"

Bubba said, "That's The Pencil's mother and the guy that fucked us up in Outerditch. Remember?"

"I don't remember," Day said.

"He didn't fuck me up," Butch said. "I'll go have a talk."

Butch strode down the beach barefoot and shirtless, leaving the others to continue their cooking preparations.

He stepped into the shade of the *palapa*. "My friends tell me you fucked them up."

"Go away and leave us alone," Wencel's mother said. "We don't want any trouble."

"No, no," Butch said, "no trouble. We're glad to be here. There's no better place anywhere. We're even getting a new store pretty soon. Welcome. We're roasting sea slugs. Would you like some?"

"Thanks, but I'm full of pizzle," Howard said.

"And we've got a little maxi if you're interested," Butch added.

Wencel's mother hoisted her bag of maximine to the table-top. "I have some, too. It's the only thing we salvaged."

"Fantastic," Butch said. "That's enough for everybody till the store gets built."

Wencel's mother said. "We're looking for some people from Outerditch. Rosy and Jimmy Junior, and maybe Wencel and Daisy."

"Yeah, we know them. Their cabin's right at the top of the big dune. They'll be down here for a swim and some slugs pretty soon. Come on over. We'll have a breakfast party."

"All right," Wencel's mother said.

"Not me," Howard said. "I'll stay here in the shade. I feel bad."

"Whatever," Butch said. "I have to go cook the slugs."

"I'll be along," Wencel's mother said.

Butch saw the radio sitting on the table under the *palapa*. "Hey, bring that radio when you come."

She attempted to ease Howard from his funk. "Howie, let's go find the kids. Don't sit there and sulk."

"Leave me alone. I've got a case of the black twirlies."

"All right, then."

She ventured out of the *palapa* and down the beach. She angled toward the water's edge, removed her tennies, and walked in the shallows to cool her feet. From there she could see two people fishing from the far arc of the jetty.

They were quite far away and she couldn't be sure, but one of them looked like Rosy. She turned back for a moment to see if Howard had stirred at all and instead saw him running toward her and pointing toward the big dune. "Look! Look at them!"

Wencel was slip-sliding down the steep face of the dune with Jimmy Junior riding on his back, Daisy and Fleadle leading the way.

Wencel's mother was overjoyed. She'd lost most everything else, but she'd found the kids.

Howard raised his fists in the air. He was giddy. "I'll build a stairway all the way up that damned thing. I'll get stones from the jetty. They won't be missed."

Wencel and Daisy were breathless when they recognized Wencel's mother and ran to her. Daisy lifted Jimmy Junior from Wencel's shoulders.

"Hello, Mother. We're glad you're here."

"We're all here, Wence. What could be better?"

Howard caught up to them. "Hey, that dune is too steep. I'm going to build a stairway. There's plenty of stones over there." He turned his head toward the jetty.

"They were thrown up by the Blast is what they told us in Pop History," Daisy said.

"Where's Rosy?" Wencel's mother asked.

"She's out there fishing with Stan Gunn if you can believe that," Jimmy Junior said.

Wencel's mother said, "*The* Stan Gunn?" She shaded her eyes. "Fishing with Rosy? I thought he died ages ago."

"No, no," Wencel said. "Just hidden from history, or lost in history. I don't remember."

"He lives right down the lane," Daisy said. "And he's going to open a store. Now that all these township people are coming here and moving into the cabins, we need a store. The old store is out of business."

"And a decent stairway," Howard said. "I'll start bringing stones over tomorrow at low tide. I won't use any mortar. It'll be one stone on top of another stone all the way up. Even Jimmy Junior'll have an easy time of it."

One of the boys waved at them. "Steaks ready! Come get some."

Howard said, "Not me. I'm full."

"Me either," Jimmy Junior said. "Thanks, but I don't eat."

Bubba passed around a bottle of bitter weed wine. "Have a drink, friends. Life is worth living at last."

Day forked slugs onto old army plates. About the size and thickness of a human palm, the steaks oozed steaming juices and smelled of rotting seaweed.

By the time the wine had gone around more than once, all but Jimmy Junior were woozy and confused.

"These slugs are delicious," Wencel's mother said. "I've never had them."

By now, Rosy and Mr. Gunn were making their way back from the far reach of the jetty and were close enough for all to see that Rosy carried a fish with a black-striped silvery body as long as her arm. Its weighty tail dragged along behind her, as did Mr. Gunn, who stepped on it now and again, slowing Rosy down.

Rosy dropped the fish in the sand when she saw Daisy. They hugged and laughed and walked away on their own to talk privately.

Mr. Gunn picked up the fish and brought it to the boys at the brazier.

"Scale it, gut it, and cook it. If you people have slug steaks on your plate, throw them in the water. We've got a drum to eat. Rosy caught it."

Wencel said, "You're Stan Gunn, the genius behind the pedway?"

"No, I'm *Stanley* Gunn. You're thinking of Stanislaus Gunn, my great grandfather."

Rosy and Daisy returned to the group. Daisy said, "Mr. Gunn, Rosy tells me your wife is completely gone."

"It's for the best," Mr. Gunn said. "We'll dig a hole tomorrow. I'm tired already and the day has barely started."

Howard waved his hammy arm and caught Mr. Gunn's attention. "When you get that store built, we'll need a stairway up that dune, Mr. Gunn. I can build it. Hell, I can build your store if you want me to."

"Come see me after I put the wife under. We'll talk about plans."

"You need help with that? I can shovel like a demon."

"Where are you staying?"

"With Jimmy Junior, Rosy, Daisy, Wencel, Wencel's mother, Howard, and Fleadle the dog."

"I know that place. I take my morning shit in their privy. Meet me there at daybreak."

"Yes, sir, I will."

By now the boys were cooking Rosy's big drum on the brazier and the wine went around again.

Wencel's mother cranked the radio and located a station in Bunkerville with a strong signal broadcasting melodies from the Age of Sinatra.

"Sinatra was a good singer," Wencel said. "We were taught that."

At mid-morning the comet dimmed and the sun beat down unmercifully. Wencel took off his school jacket. When he did, he heard his father's teeth rattle.

"Mother, what should I do with these?" He held the remaining seven in his open hand for her to see.

"I don't care. Throw them in the water." She had a sip of wine and passed the bottle to Howard.

Wencel went as close to the lapping waves as he could without getting his shoes wet and flung the teeth out with all his strength. Fleadle ran a little way into the water after the teeth, stopped, thought better of it, and turned back.

"The drum's cooked," Butch said. "Let's eat."